HIP HOP KIDZ®

Bring It On

Not any more

~~Bree T. Williams~~

Gabrielle

HiP HoP KiDZ®

Bring It On

Written by Jasmine Beller

Bree T. Williams

Grosset & Dunlap

GROSSET & DUNLAP
Published by the Penguin Group
Penguin Group (USA) Inc., 375 Hudson Street, New York,
New York 10014, U.S.A.
Penguin Group (Canada), 90 Eglinton Avenue East, Suite 700,
Toronto, Ontario, Canada M4P 2Y3
(a division of Pearson Penguin Canada Inc.)
Penguin Books Ltd, 80 Strand, London WC2R 0RL, England
Penguin Ireland, 25 St Stephen's Green, Dublin 2, Ireland
(a division of Penguin Books Ltd)
Penguin Group (Australia), 250 Camberwell Road, Camberwell,
Victoria 3124, Australia
(a division of Pearson Australia Group Pty Ltd)
Penguin Books India Pvt Ltd, 11 Community Centre, Panchsheel Park,
New Delhi - 110 017, India
Penguin Group (NZ), Cnr Airborne and Rosedale Roads, Albany,
Auckland 1310, New Zealand
(a division of Pearson New Zealand Ltd)
Penguin Books (South Africa) (Pty) Ltd, 24 Sturdee Avenue,
Rosebank, Johannesburg 2196, South Africa

Penguin Books Ltd, Registered Offices:
80 Strand, London WC2R 0RL, England

Library of Congress Control Number: 2006007604.

ISBN 0-448-44362-7   10 9 8 7 6 5 4 3 2 1

CHAPTER 1

Devane—that's right, no last name—studied the extra-large calendar that took up most of the wall space in her bedroom. Make that her *half* of the bedroom. The other half belonged to her little brother, Tamal. Tamal Edwards. Who, at this very moment, was eating a PB&J with one hand and drawing some anime-style cartoon with the other and not even noticing that he was getting the J all over the paper. Unlike Devane, Tamal would definitely have to use his last name his whole life long. Last name *and* middle initial.

What Devane knew and Tamal didn't was that if you were gonna be a star of any kind, you had to have a plan. Tamal L. Edwards was only two years younger than Devane. He was already in the fifth grade. But he had no plan whatsoever. He couldn't even plan far enough ahead to get a napkin when he was eating a sandwich.

But Tamal wasn't Devane's problem. Devane had to concentrate on Devane. And according to her giant calendar,

Devane had a big day ahead of her. Today—July 20—was circled on her calendar with the red glitter pen she used for make-or-break days. If she triumphed at the Hip Hop Kidz audition, the one in less than two hours, she'd be right on schedule in her three-year plan for world domination.

Yeah, yeah, yeah, today wasn't supposed to be an "audition." But come on, people, that's what it was. Maddy Caulder, the creative director of Hip Hop Kidz, was making the rounds, observing all the basic Hip Hop Kidz classes, looking to pick new dancers for the Hip Hop Kidz Performance Group.

And in that group Devane would be *seen*. She wouldn't be hiding her stuff in the classroom. She'd be out in front of an audience.

Devane flipped on her CD player, flooding the tiny space with Missy Elliott's "Lose Control." Her girl had served it up with that one, and the music was exactly what Devane needed to get her into the power zone.

"Not Missy," Tamal groaned. "Not *Miiissssy*."

Devane ignored him. She began to pump her body, imagining herself in the "Lose Control" video. That was the second step in her plan of world domination—her own video. First, she'd become the star of the Hip Hop Kidz Performance Group. Of course she'd get in. There was no one Devane-worthy in her class to get in the way.

Maybe Ky Miggs, this guy who'd been a steamin' b-ball

player at her school until he wrecked his wrist. Ky was in one of the other basic classes, and his moves were *almost* as good as hers. But Devane didn't have to sweat him. Maddy needed guys *and* girls for the Performance Group.

That meant the let's-not-call-it-an-audition audition was bagged. And *that* meant she was all that much closer to livin' large. Videos. Choreography jobs. MTV awards. Acting jobs. Oscars. Directing. More Oscars. Producing. And . . . a rainstorm of cash and cars. Not that she was going to go all mad car disease, but she needed enough cars that she'd never have to shove herself into another reekin' city bus. Enough cars so that her mother wouldn't have to spend half her life commuting to her three jobs on the bus, either.

Even Tamal wouldn't have to take the bus ever again in life—unless he got all foolish. Then he could bus it until he shaped himself up.

Silence slammed into the room. Devane was jerked away from her daydreams. She was back in the bedroom—back in real life. The smell of her brother's sandwich filled her nose. The summer air coming in from the window felt like it was sweating, like it was sweating all over her body. Was the air everywhere in Miami as nasty as it was in Overtown? Or did the rich people in Hibiscus Island have bottled O2 to go with their bottled water?

Devane shook her head and smiled at the thought of bottles of air filling up designer purses and briefcases. Then she put on an extreme frown and turned to her brother. "Tell me you didn't just turn off Missy," she said, trying to sound scary. She didn't want Little B to start thinking he could get away with stunts like killing her music.

He grinned. "I didn't just turn off Missy."

"You'll be takin' the bus for a very long time unless you do some serious booty kissing," she muttered. She grabbed her gym bag and her Kmart MP3 player, which sounded just as good as an iPod and was nearly as fly. She'd get to the dance studio early and score some no-little-brother practice time in one of the rooms that wasn't being used. Not that she needed more practice. She'd been getting ready for this day since 2001, when she became Devane. Just Devane. No last name necessary.

"How bizarre is it that they make camouflage in orange and purple, anyway? Where would they really help you blend in? A convention of clowns?" Sophie Qian asked her older sister.

Sammi laughed. "True. But you don't want to blend in at all at the Hip Hop Kidz audition." She studied the explosion of clothes on Sophie's bed. "So the purple-and-orange camouflage pants. Definitely. Straight out of the hip-hop fashion bible."

Sophie pulled on the pants. They had the Sammi seal of

approval. That was all Sophie needed to hear. Sammi was chosen Most Fashion Forward at school last year, when she was an eighth grader. Had her picture in the yearbook for it. And for being a cheerleader. And for being on the honor roll. And for being in choir. And for being class VP. It would be easy to hate Sammi . . . if Sammi wasn't impossible to hate.

Although Sophie did get an attack of the jealouses every once in a while. But that wouldn't happen if she made it into the Performance Group. Then Sophie would have something, too, the way Sammi had cheerleading, and choir, and honor roll, and *and* and *and* and *and*. Her sister added something new to the list of things to be oohed and aahed over by the parents and everybody else what felt like every other day.

"Sophie, if you want a ride in my cab, move it," her father called from the living room. "I need some paying customers today."

"Three more secs," Sophie called back. "How 'bout my lucky Trix rabbit shirt to go with?" she asked Sammi.

"Very nice," Sammi agreed.

Sophie tugged on the shirt and checked herself out in the mirror. She looked good, she decided. She still looked thick. But she couldn't expect the pants to camouflage that away. Because if she was honest, she had to admit she was maybe more fat than thick, although it depended on who you asked. There were a couple of high school guys in her neighborhood who looked at her funny. But the guys at Miami Springs Middle School, where Sophie was in the sixth grade? Not so much. They joked around with Sophie, came to her for advice about other girls, asked her for her sister's phone number—but seemed to have no idea she even had legs at all.

"Sophie!" their dad yelled.

"Let me help with that," Sammi said as Sophie started working her thick black hair into a bunch of knotted twists with the ends sticking out. "Dad's about to go to Defcon 1."

"Thanks. I need to get water to bring." Sophie headed for the kitchen, Sammi half a step behind her, continuing to do her hair magic.

"All done," Sammi said, clipping Sophie's last hair twist into place. "You look amazing. You're gonna burn today."

"I'll be sure to tell everyone who dressed me when I'm on the red carpet," Sophie promised as she grabbed a package of Ding Dongs from her stash behind her mom's never-run-out double row of paper towels in the top cupboard. "Want one?" she asked Sammi.

"No thanks."

Sophie slid the Dings into one of the giganto pockets of her cargo pants. "I'm ready to go, Dad." She headed for the front door and led the way down the stairs of their flamingo-pink apartment building.

"You want to borrow the lucky horse from my key chain? Or the fir tree air freshener?" her father asked after they'd gotten in the cab.

Sophie laughed. "I don't think I'm gonna stink up the place that much, Dad."

"I didn't mean it like that. Your sister wore it around her neck for good luck in that talent show," he protested.

"When she was five," Sophie reminded him.

"It's just that there are a lot of kids in the basic classes, right?" her dad asked. "That means a lot of competition to get into the Performance Group. And, you know, it's not all about talent. Being a performer takes a certain look."

A skinnier-than-Sophie look? Is that what he means? Sophie wondered, unwrapping the Ding Dong.

She shook her head. *He just doesn't want you to be disappointed, that's all.*

"I'll take the horse," she answered. "But isn't it supposed to be the good luck charm for lotteries? Or am I getting my Chinese folklore mixed up again? I know, I know, I should pay closer attention when you and Mom talk about our heritage."

"It is for lotteries, but I figure, close enough," her father said.

"Works for me," Sophie agreed. "And I'll take whatever help I can get to be a Hip Hop Kid."

Emerson Lane smiled when she saw that the driver of the Town Car was Vincent. Vincent liked to talk—and not on the cell, like some of the younger guys. He liked talking to Emerson. The long drive from Hibiscus Island to the Hip Hop Kidz rehearsal space was so boring without him.

"Are you nervous about your audition this afternoon?" Vincent asked as he opened the car door for her. Vincent talked *and* he listened *and* he remembered. Even her parents didn't always manage that combination.

"It's not exactly an audition," Emerson told him.

"Oh, excuse me. I thought when you did your stuff and then people decided if they wanted you in some kind of Performance Group, it was called an audition." He winked at her, his dark brown eyes crinkling at the corners. "But I didn't go to the Miami Country Day School like you. My vocabulary must not be that good," he said, then shut the door with a light click.

"So are you nervous?" Vincent asked again as he got behind the wheel.

"Of course." There was no reason to pretend with Vincent. He'd been driving her around since she was six, and she was thirteen now. Even when she broke her leg right before the Jamison Ballet Intensive audition, she'd admitted to him that she was almost glad that the break got her out of going to that audition. A truth her mother could've never tolerated.

It wasn't that Emerson didn't love ballet. She did. She'd loved it since she played the littlest mouse in the *Nutcracker* when she was five. But for almost a year, for months and months before she'd broken her leg, she'd kept on getting the impulse to bust out, just let the music fill her and let her body . . . go. Not something that would have been encouraged at the Jamison Intensive. But something that was very encouraged at the Hip Hop Kidz classes she'd ended up taking instead.

"You're gonna rock the house," Vincent told her.

Emerson loved it when Vincent talked street. Not all fifty-plus men could pull it off, but he could. "You've never even seen me dance," Emerson protested.

Vincent met her gaze in the rearview mirror. "Doesn't matter. I've seen the way you look when you come out of your classes. You really love hip-hop, am I right?"

"Mm-hmm. It's looser than ballet. It's like I'm not even myself when I'm dancing hip-hop."

"I think it's just the opposite. I think that's when you're the full-on Emerson," Vincent answered.

The full-on Emerson. Emerson wasn't even sure if she knew who that person was.

"Good luck," Vincent said as he pulled up in front of the studio. "Not that I think you need it."

"Thanks. And I'll get the door," she added quickly, even though Vincent already knew that. She always asked him to let her open the door herself at Hip Hop Kidz. It was bad enough that she had a driver; she didn't need to rub it in people's faces by having him wait on her.

"I'll be right here," Vincent said.

"Okay, bye!" Emerson grabbed her dance bag and jumped out of the car. She spotted Sophie Qian bopping toward the studio door.

"Em, hey!" Sophie called.

"Hi!" Emerson called back.

"Come on. We're early enough to check out the competition for a couple of minutes." Sophie covered her mouth. "Oops. I didn't say *competition*, did I? That wasn't me, was it? Because all that's happening today are some *regular, ordinary* Hip Hop Kidz basic dance classes, right? But there isn't any reason we can't watch the *regular, ordinary class* before ours as long as they *don't* audition, is there?"

Emerson grinned. There wasn't any reason to answer—Sophie would just keep talking. Sophie talked even more than Vincent. And that's what Emerson liked so much about her. Sometimes Emerson felt like she should sit down and write the girl a nice thank-you note for making it so easy to step into the studio or the locker room. Sophie was always friendly to everybody, always said hi and chatted with who-ever was around like she'd known them forever. It was pretty much impossible to be shy around her.

And Emerson *was* shy. It usually just didn't show that much. That's because she'd known everyone at the Miami Country Day School—and their nannies and parents, too—since she was practically prenatal. Every girl who was in her ballet class went to Country, except one. Every girl at her church went to Country. Emerson's violin teacher had given lessons to Emerson's mother. The principal had been her dad's first-grade teacher.

Hip Hop Kidz was the only place she was faced with anyone new.

Sophie opened the door to the studio and ushered Emerson through. "Looks like a few other people got the same idea," she said, jerking her chin toward the observation windows of the largest classroom. Four kids from their class were gathered around it, including even ill papi. Who probably had zero to worry about when it came to being selected for the Performance Group.

Ill papi was practically famous. Everybody knew who he was because everyone knew his dad. *Everybody.*

Well, not people like Emerson's parents. But everybody who knew even the ABCs of hip-hop knew that ill papi's father was J-Bang, one of *the* old skool dudes like Rubber Band and Kool Herc, the ones who practically invented the style of dancing. The buzz was that ill papi was the new skool version of his dad, just as cutting edge, just as much of a rule breaker. Of course, ill papi was in the Performance Group.

"How many girls do you think want to get into the group just so they can hang with ill papi?" Sophie whispered. "I'm guessing thirty-five percent. And he's a big bonus for another forty," she said, answering her own question.

Ill papi turned toward a guy from their class and laughed, giving Emerson a good look at his deep brown eyes, his light caramel skin, and the dimple on one side of his mouth. She thought he was about a year older than she was. Probably going into ninth grade. "I'd say you're right," Emerson agreed.

Sophie snorted. "People always say to dance your passion." She headed down to the windows with Emerson right behind her. "Buddha driving a Volkswagen, as my grandmother would say," Sophie breathed. "Look at that girl go."

Emerson didn't have to ask which girl. It was completely, totally, absolutely obvious. The African American girl who was doing flares with her *legs crossed*. The whole class was down on the floor doing flares. Standard flares. And they were hard enough—bracing your weight on your hands and swinging your legs through the air and around your body. But doing the move with your legs crossed was hugely more difficult. Emerson could do a flare with her legs together, but that was as far as she'd gotten.

"I'd say she's had a little too much fun with her Bedazzler.

I mean, the T-shirt. But other than that, she's awesome," Sophie commented.

"That's Devane," volunteered Leeza, a girl from Sophie and Emerson's class, not taking her eyes off the window.

Devane.

Devane is definitely getting picked for the Performance Group, Emerson thought. *How could she not?*

How many girls did the group need? More than just Devane? Did Emerson have a shot? Even the full-on Emerson?

CHAPTER 2

"Meet the newest member of the Performance Group!" Devane called out as she strolled into the locker room, her brown eyes sparkling. "The name's Devane. But you can call me Divine if you want to," she went on. "Divine, but not Diva. I'm not gonna be asking anybody to fetch me a wide selection of mineral waters or M&M's with all the green ones picked out, at least not until I get my first MTV award."

Emerson's heart turned to a big piece of lead in her chest as she pulled on her track pants. She'd expected Devane to make the group. But wouldn't Maddy at least wait and see everybody in all the classes before she made her choice?

"Wait. Back up. Ms. Caulder already told you you're in?" Sophie asked the question Emerson was afraid to. Sophie wasn't afraid to say anything.

Leeza looked up, eager to hear the answer, too.

I hope Sophie makes it into the Performance Group, Emerson thought. *Fearlessness should be rewarded.*

"Nah. But you saw me in there," Devane answered with a

grin. "Think I didn't notice all of you with your noses pressed against the window when I did my flare? Are you saying you don't think I'm a lock?"

"Not saying anything. Just asking," Sophie told her.

The muscles in Emerson's shoulders relaxed a little. The decision to put Devane in the Performance Group wasn't actually official. At least not yet. Her muscles tensed back up as she bent over to tie her shoes.

Devane leaned against the closest row of lockers. "So I need some help. Pretty soon I'll be starring in a music video, then comes the cash."

Emerson caught sight of two girls from Devane's class exchanging a *can-you-believe-her?* look. Devane had done some amazing dancing. But didn't she realize that she was basically saying that she was better than everybody else in the room? Didn't she understand that that was just . . . rude?

"What do you think I should get first?" Devane didn't wait for an answer. "A little dog in a coat, like Paris Hilton's dog? Or the stretch SUV? Or the movie-star boyfriend?"

Everybody laughed. It was impossible not to. Devane kept her face completely serious, but it was clear she was just messing with them.

Emerson pulled the lace of her left sneaker tight, and it snapped. She grimaced. "Sophie. Do you have a safety pin or anything?" she whispered.

Devane narrowed her eyes and straightened up. "Hey,

Blondie. If you're gonna say something, make it loud enough for the whole class to hear," she told Emerson.

"I just said I needed a pin," Emerson answered. She glanced at Sophie, wondering if she was imagining the attitude suddenly radiating off Divine Devane.

Devane took a step closer to Emerson and ran her eyes from Emerson's blond ponytail to the tips of her sneakers. "Are you sure you're in the right place?" Devane asked. "This isn't the locker room for hollaback girls."

Emerson wanted to say something to Devane. But her brain had just gone liquid.

She yanked her broken lace out of the top two holes and tied it down lower. "I'm a dancer, not a cheerleader," she finally managed to get out. "And this is exactly where I belong." She hurried out of the locker room before Devane could toss out something else that would make Emerson's brain go mushy and went straight to the practice room.

She calmed down a little the second she stepped inside. This really was exactly where she belonged. It was her favorite place in the world. Not this specific practice room. Any practice room. The wood floor. The mirrors. The faint smell of sweat that never went away. She loved it all.

Emerson suddenly had to move. Just had to.

She went into a locking arabesque, something she'd never tried before. Just the basic ballet move, but freeze-framed into a hundred little pieces that lasted only a split second each.

She was so into the motion that at first she didn't realize Sophie had entered the room. Then she spotted Sophie watching her, leaning back, arms crossed.

When Emerson finished, Sophie gave an exaggerated nod, then did a version of the arabesque herself but more clown style than the basic locking Emerson had chosen. There were times Sophie moved so fast her arms and legs blurred and moments where her whole body quivered like mini-earthquakes were running through it. Sophie finished up and shot Emerson an expectant look.

Uh-oh. Sophie wanted to battle. That definitely wasn't a ballet class kind of thing. The hip-hop arabesque she'd just tried out was the first time she'd let go and attempted a move that wasn't part of the choreography that their teacher, Randall, laid out. All her blabbing to Vincent about how much looser hip-hop was . . . that was pretty much just blabbing. In theory it was true, but Emerson hadn't truly put the theory into practice. She usually stood against the wall until Randall came in and started class, then she followed his instructions exactly.

Sophie cleared her throat, that I'm-waiting sound. *The me who broke out with the arabesque, maybe she's the full-on me Vincent was talking about,* Emerson thought.

"Bring it to her, Emerson," Ky Miggs called from his spot leaning next to the CD player. Emerson hadn't even heard him come in. She was kind of surprised he knew her name, even though they'd been in class together for a few months.

"Yeah, you're not burned already, are you?" Leeza asked. Emerson hadn't heard her come in either.

She had a choice. She could scurry back to her usual spot against the wall. Or she could do battle.

Emerson closed her eyes for a moment. Feeling the beat, letting it take hold of her body, set the rhythm the way her heart usually did. Her muscles and sinews and bones wanted to *go*. And she let them. She launched into a locking pirouette, then flipped down into a 1990. She got about a half spin on one hand before she had to flip herself back to her feet again. Emerson didn't know how the high-spin, low-spin combo looked. In her head it looked great. And it felt incredible.

She shot a glance at her audience of two. Her heart lurched into her throat as she saw that three more kids had joined the group. And so had Maddy. They were all smiling at her. All of them. Maddy was *smiling* at her.

"Now what you got, Soph?" Ky called.

Emerson started to turn back toward Sophie and realized there was another person watching. Devane. The girl stood outside the room, looking in through the window. She wasn't smiling. She was looking right at Emerson, her mouth twisted into a scowl.

It's like she hates me, Emerson thought.

"And five, six, seven, eight!" Randall called. "Now we throw the pizza dough, throw the pizza dough."

Sophie put her hands up in the air and got her hips moving. She loved the way Randall described the moves in their routines. He was so goofy.

"Okay, and surfer on a smooth wave." Randall undulated his abdomen in an easy, fluid motion.

Sophie let the smooth wave roll from her sternum down through her core to her hips. She felt her Ding Dongs dancing along inside her. She probably shouldn't have eaten quite so close to class.

Being a performer takes a certain look.

Her father's words jolted through her brain, and she fell out of rhythm with the rest of the group. Did Maddy see? Sophie cut a sideways glance at her. Didn't seem like she had. And this was basically just the warm-up. She wasn't going to pick who got in the Performance Group based on the warm-up, right?

"Rough waves, now. Rough wave, rough wave!" Randall instructed.

Sophie let the rough wave shoot all the way through her body, jerking her muscles in order from her neck down to her feet. She tried to focus all her attention on dancing. But a little piece of her brain was busy checking out all the other bodies in the class. Categorizing. Plus size. Minus size. King. Queen. Regular. Supersize me. Kiddie meal. Papa bear. Mama bear. Baby bear.

There are all thicknesses in here, Dad, she thought. Like her father was a mind reader and he'd get her message out in his cab wherever he was. She left out the fact that the only person in class who was actually bigger than her was a boy.

Didn't matter. There was a girl her size in the Performance Group. Sophie had seen her, and she owned the stage.

"Next up, broncos," Randall called. "Four of them."

Sophie dropped down on her hands and kicked her legs up behind her like a bucking bronc. *What if one big girl is all Ms. Caulder wants in the group?* she thought as she sprang back to her feet.

Big girl. That was one of Sophie's mother's expressions. She actually hauled out *such a pretty face,* too. Those actual words.

This is not the time to start listening to your parents, Sophie told herself.

She decided to practice a little Jedi mind control on Ms. Caulder instead. *See me. See Sophie. See my moves. Don't just see my big booty. See* Sophie.

CHAPTER 3

"Everyone was looking at me," Sammi told her family at the dinner table. She stabbed one green bean with her fork and ate it. "I never taught a cheerleading routine by myself, but since I'm head cheerleader when school starts up, I have to get used to it, so I volunteered. And it was actually pretty fun. Who knew I was such a control freak?"

"Um, everyone?" Sophie joked.

"Sophie, that's not nice," her mother said. *Nice* was very big with their mom.

"I didn't mean it mean. Sammi knows that," Sophie answered. "I just meant my lovely and talented older sister wouldn't be able to do all the stuff she does if she wasn't a little bit type A."

Her father snorted. "People say type A like it's a bad thing. I call it type Ambition." He glanced at his watch. "Speaking of—I have about five more minutes before I have to get myself and my cab back on the street."

"Let me get out the Tupperware and pack up some of

your dinner," Sophie's mom said. Mom loved Tupperware almost as much as she loved *nice*. She sold it at parties, but Sophie suspected her mother would still have the parties even if she didn't make any money just so she could show people how awesome Tupperware was. "You'll get indigestion if you—"

She was interrupted by the phone ringing. Sammi leapt for it. No one else even twitched. Sammi got more calls than Sophie, her mom, and her dad combined. Calls from friends wanting to hook up. Calls from people needing homework help. Calls from cheerleaders on her squad. Calls from other kids in her choir. And calls from guys, guys, guys, and oh, yeah, more guys.

"Sophie, it's for you." Sammi handed her the cordless phone and sat back down.

"Talk to me," Sophie said into the phone. Her dad smiled at the greeting, and her mother shook her head, trying not to smile.

"Hello? Sophie? It's Maddy Caulder."

Sophie sat up so straight, she added three inches to her height. "Maddy?" she chirped at a pitch high enough to puncture a dog's eardrum. "Hi. Hello."

Why don't you just add "hola," "ni hao," and "howdy" while you're at it? Sophie thought to herself with a grimace.

Sammi reached out and grabbed Sophie's hand. Sophie squeezed back, glad to have someone to hang on to.

"I enjoyed watching you in your class today," Maddy said.

Please, please, pleasepleaseplease, let me be in, Sophie thought. *I'll give up Ding Dongs. No, okay, I'm lying. But BBQ corn chips. Really. Or my Bo Bice poster, if that would be better.*

"You've really got something special, a great sense of playfulness," Maddy continued. "So I'm inviting you to join the Performance Group!"

"Woo-hoo! The Bo poster's coming right down!" Sophie cried.

"What?" Maddy asked.

"Nothing. I mean, thanks. I would love to. So, so much," Sophie told her.

"I'd like you to think it over. It's a big commitment. I need to know that you'll be able to attend all the group classes and the extra rehearsals for performances. I'd like to go over the requirements with one of your parents so you can make the decision together."

"Oh. Um, okay." Sophie thrust the phone at her mother. "Talk to Ms. Caulder. She's the head of Hip Hop Kidz. I got in the Performance Group. Whatever she asks, just say yes!"

"You got in?" Sammi squealed, tightening her grip on Sophie's hand until Sophie thought some of the little bones might snap.

"Yep, I got in!" Sophie jumped up and started doing a

King Tut strut over to her father. "Dad, I got in!"

"Congratulations!" he said into her ear as he gave her a hug.

Does he sound surprised? Just a little surprised? Sophie tried to shove the thought away. This should be a happy-thought-only moment.

"What a lucky guy I am!" he added. "Both my daughters are winners."

He definitely didn't sound surprised now. Just proud of her. Sophie spun away from him. She needed to *move*. She added some poppin' to her King Tut as she headed into the living room, jerking her head forward and back like a snake that kept starting to strike and changing its mind.

Sammi ran past her and punched on the radio. Their mom's fave, Harry Connick, Jr., started singing about . . . something old. Sophie thought she'd unprogrammed the "lite" station. Clearly their mother had found it again. But even the extreme bad flava of the music couldn't damage her mood. She was in the Performance Group. She kept on poppin' right along with Mr. Mellow. Sammi joined in, doing some of her cheerleader moves.

It'll be so perfect, Sophie thought. *Now we'll both have something of our own. Well, Sammi will have about fifty somethings. But I'll have one really amazing one. I'll be on stage with the Hip Hop Kidz!*

Just tell them what Ms. Caulder said about Hip Hop Kidz, Emerson told herself. *It'll be okay.*

She'd been giving herself this advice since the salad course, and now her parents were on coffee and Emerson was pretending to eat a scoop of mango sorbet. She was afraid to actually eat it. The rest of her dinner felt like it had turned to cement inside her stomach. If she put anything else down there, she might never be able to stand up.

They expect excellence in everything, she thought. *They live for excellence. This won't be any different.*

Emerson's mouth was so dry, her tongue was stuck to the roof of her mouth. If she tried to speak right now, her words would come out thick and garbled. That wouldn't be the way to start off this conversation.

She took a sip of her water. *Now, before your tongue gets stuck again. Before Mom has to find a speaker for the next DAR luncheon or do the seating chart for some benefit,* she ordered herself. *Before Dad heads for his study to work.* Even though Emerson could never figure out what an anesthesiologist did in his home office.

"Class was good today," she blurted out, a little too loud and a lot too fast. Emerson and her parents didn't share enough vocabulary for her to explain what they actually *did* in class. *Jetes,* they got. *Flares,* they didn't. *Chasse,* yes. Float, no. "Maddy Caulder, the director of the program, stopped by to observe," Emerson added, more calmly and slowly. "She phoned a little while ago, before either of you got home. She'd like to talk to one of you."

Oops. She hadn't meant to say that part yet.

"Record messages like that on voice mail, so there's no confusion," her mother said.

Emerson nodded. "Right. I will." She cleared her throat. The dryness was taking over again. "She wants to talk to you because she'd like me to join the Hip Hop Kidz Performance Group."

Her parents exchanged a look. One of those looks that was a whole conversation. Then her mother opened her mouth to speak.

"She thinks my dancing is really strong. Excellent, in fact. It's a great opportunity," Emerson added, not exactly interrupting, but almost. "And it would look great on my transcripts. The group performs all over. They've opened for—well, for singers you've never heard of."

Her father raised one eyebrow. "The Backstreet Boys," he guessed.

"Um. Sort of," Emerson answered. Her dad didn't like to be told he'd never heard of something. But he really didn't know hip-hop music. "They do stuff for charity, too. Like nursing homes and the United Heart Association," she added, locking eyes with her mom.

Her parents had another little eye talk. "It sounds as if it might be fairly time-consuming," her mother said. "During the summer it's one thing. But when school starts again, you'll need to get back to your study schedule. We're getting you a French tutor this year, remember."

"And what about ballet?" her father asked. "That broken leg kept you out of the Intensive, but you're still having your regular lessons."

She *had* still been taking her regular lessons. But the class for the kids in the hip-hop Performance Group actually met on exactly the same day as her ballet class. At exactly the same time. She decided not to mention that detail quite yet.

"And I love ballet!" Emerson answered. And she did. She just loved hip-hop in a different way.

"I would hope so, considering I've been paying for the lessons almost since you could walk," her dad answered. "Won't you be performing in the *Nutcracker* again this year?"

Emerson nibbled on her lip. This was getting out of control. She probably would be selected to perform in the professional company of the *Nutcracker*—if she was still taking her ballet classes. The company always used some local students in their production. But even now, in July, she could imagine almost exactly what steps she would be doing in the show. This year she'd be a snowflake. Which would be fun . . . but predictable.

All that cement in her stomach broke apart—into big hard rocks. They slammed around inside her. She could already see how this was going to go. Ballet and the *Nutcracker* would win. Emerson was going to have to tell Maddy no.

Or she was going to have to convince her parents to change their minds.

And the last time she'd attempted that had been . . . pretty much never.

"What if I don't perform in the *Nutcracker?*" she asked, leaving the issue of missing the actual ballet classes for later. "I've done it seven years in a row. I really love the hip-hop classes. And the Performance Group is fantastic. You should see them. And like I said, it would be something great for my transcripts. Something in addition to the ballet with the *Nutcracker, Nutcracker, Nutcracker.* Colleges appreciate diversity."

"They also appreciate consistency," her mother answered. "And it's part of our holiday tradition to see you in the performance."

It's part of our holiday tradition for the two of us to get our picture in the society page together, Emerson thought. *Me in my* Nutcracker *costume. You smiling proudly. Followed by a nice little blurb about all your hard work during the year on the Arts Council.* She hoped the little burst of anger that had come with the thought hadn't shown on her face.

Her father sighed. "Honey, we really weren't satisfied with where you were academically last year. Miami Country Day School expects a lot of its students, and your school-work has to come first."

"French was the only big problem," Emerson protested. "And we all—you, me, and Mom—came up with a fix for that. I'm going to have a tutor, starting on day one of school in September. I'm not going to have any chance to fall behind." She sucked in a deep breath. "I really want this. And you've both always told me if I really want something, I should do what I have to do to get it."

Her parents had another eye conversation. Why couldn't they use words? She could fight words. Sort of. For the millionth time, she wished she had a brother or sister. Some-one to have her own eye conversations with. Someone to take her side.

"I'm sorry," her mother said. "We understand how important hip-hop is to you. But you've put so much time and effort into your ballet. You don't want to waste it."

"And you're so talented," her father added. "You'll be happy one day that you stuck with it and really gave it your full-out effort."

"You mean *you'll* be happy that I stuck with it," Emerson blurted out before it even registered that she was talking back to her parents.

"Emerson—your father and I don't like that kind

of talk. And one can only wonder where your attitude is coming from. Though I wouldn't be at all surprised if it came from those Hip Hop Kidz," said Mrs. Lane before turning to Mr. Lane and asking him a question about the neighbors' garden.

And with that, Emerson knew the case was officially closed. She stared down at her sorbet and gave the pink puddle of mush a halfhearted stir. "May I be excused?" she asked. "I need to call Maddy and tell her so that she can choose someone else."

Her mother nodded, and Emerson laid her napkin next to her plate, then slowly made her way upstairs to her bedroom and sat down at her cherrywood desk. There was nothing to do but call Maddy.

Emerson forced herself to pick up her dance bag. She had the card with Maddy's number inside. But the first thing she saw when she unzipped the bag was the scrap of paper with Sophie's number on it. She and Sophie had exchanged numbers after the "audition" so they could call each other if either of them heard anything.

Impulsively Emerson grabbed her pale blue phone—bought to match the sable-moonlight duvet cover her mother had picked out for her bed—and dialed the number.

"Talk to me," someone said into her ear. Emerson was pretty sure it was Sophie. But she wasn't positive.

"May I speak to Sophie, please?" she asked.

"You are," Sophie said. "Hey, two calls for me in one night! Are you jealous, Sammi?" she joked to someone in the room with her. "Who is this?" she asked into the phone.

"It's Emerson."

"Em! I was gonna call you! Did you get in?" Sophie demanded.

"Yes," Emerson said, her voice cracking.

"And you're so happy, you've been moved to tears?" Sophie asked.

Emerson hardly knew Sophie. They never talked about important stuff. But all it took was that one question from Sophie—and everything came spilling out of Emerson. Her broken leg. The *Nutcracker.* The French tutor. How she felt when she danced hip-hop.

"Wow," Sophie said when she finished.

"I know," Emerson answered. "Right now, the way I feel, I'd just call Maddy up myself and pretend to be my mom. But I'm afraid she'd recognize my voice. Or at least know I'm a kid."

She could hardly believe those words had come out of her mouth. But she meant it. Her parents just didn't get how important hip-hop was to her. They never would. The only way she'd be able to stay in the Performance Group was to lie to them. And to Maddy.

"If that's really all that's stopping you, I could probably help," Sophie answered. "I have an older sister, and she . . .

likes to talk on the phone. We could try it."

Emerson's heart stopped beating. "Really?"

"I'm pretty sure," Sophie answered.

Emerson's heart started beating triple time. "But what if she got caught? Aren't you afraid of getting in trouble?"

"She won't get caught. We'll call from our home phone—it has a blocked ID. And my sister's a pro. She once pretended to be her best friend and called this guy she had a crush on to find out if he liked her back. This will be child's play next to that little feat."

"But why would you do that for me?" Emerson asked.

"Oh, I don't know . . . because I like you? Because I want a friend in the group? Because if I ever drop the weight, I'd like to go shopping for clothes in *your* closet?" Sophie said. "Hang tight. I'll call you back as soon as it's done." Sophie hung up.

Emerson gripped the phone with both hands and sat on the chair, motionless.

This was wrong. This was insane.

If this worked, it would be the best thing that she'd ever decided to do.

Five minutes passed. Ten. Eleven. Twelve. Emerson felt like her nerve endings were trying to dig their way out of her skin.

The phone rang. Emerson hit the Answer button. "Sophie?" she exclaimed, forgetting her phone manners.

"You're in, baby," Sophie told her. "Now listen, be careful with that white peasant blouse you were wearing the other day. Because as soon as I'm down to a size triple zero, I'm borrowing it from you, and I don't want it all covered up in ketchup stains or nothin' . . ."

"Can I? Can I? Can I?" Tamal asked. "Can I? Can I?"

"All right! All right! All right!" Devane exclaimed, too tired to say "no" one more time. "Just leave a piece for Mom."

"Oh, sweet mama, I get cake!" Tamal leaned down and took a bite. Didn't cut a slice. Didn't even use a fork. Repulsive.

"And please don't slobber over every piece," Devane exclaimed. "I didn't bake that for you." She grabbed a knife and cut the cake down the middle, evening out the mess Tamal had made. Then she carved out his ragged clump, dumped it on a plate, and pushed it toward him.

"You baked it for yourself. To tell yourself how great yourself is." Tamal used a fork to eat the next bite.

"Mom would have made it for me if she didn't have to work," Devane said.

At least she would have wanted to. She used to make cakes every time she wanted to congratulate Devane or Tamal for something. But after their dad died, their mom didn't have much time for baking. She was always at work. Like tonight. She wasn't supposed to be at the hospital, but an extra shift opened up, and her mom took it. She never said no.

Devane hadn't even gotten to tell her mother the divine news yet. Not that Mom would be surprised. She was always telling Devane what a fantastic dancer she was.

"They should have picked me," Tamal said. "I should have my own video." He started spazzing out, jerking his body around, thinking he was actually dancing. Oh, Lord. She shouldn't have let him have sugar—he was enough of a pain in the butt without it.

"Tamal, finish your cake, brush your teeth, and go to bed," Devane told him.

"You're not the boss of me."

"Fine. But let me ask you this—is Mom going to be happy if she gets home and you're shaking your bonbon around the kitchen an hour past your bedtime?"

"An hour past *my* bedtime is *your* bedtime," Tamal reminded her.

"She's gonna want to hear what I have to say to her. She won't mind if I stay up," Devane answered.

But by the time her mother came home, Devane had fallen asleep with her head on the kitchen table.

CHAPTER 4

Emerson scanned the room—in what she hoped wasn't an obvious way—as she walked into her first class with the Hip Hop Kidz Performance Group. She could hardly believe this had worked. She could hardly believe Sophie's sister had pulled off the phone call with Maddy.

She recognized a bunch of people from the one time she'd seen the group perform, including a tall guy in a Gator baseball hat. M.J., his name was. He'd had an amazing solo, and she'd looked him up in the program.

Emerson realized her scan had turned into a stare, and she forced her eyes away. A skinny girl almost as tall as M.J. with short dyed black hair and ultra-pale skin was doing stretches over in one corner. She met Emerson's gaze and smiled as she leaned over flat-backed, with her arms out in front of her. It felt like sort of an invitation, so Emerson headed over to the girl and started doing some ankle rolls. It felt better to be doing something in the room full of strangers than just standing there.

"You're one of the new meat patties. I'm Chloe," the girl said. "I hope you're ready to be tortured. I've been in the group for a year, and my muscles haven't stopped aching yet."

"Emerson. Hi." Emerson switched over to shoulder shrugs. "I'm so excited that I got in. I've only been doing hip-hop a few months. But I've been doing ballet forever."

"Ballet. I did that for about half a minute when I was little. I think it was my mom's way of trying to get me to like pink. Didn't work—obviously," Chloe answered. "I'm gonna go fill up my water bottle. You should, too, if yours isn't maxed. You'll need it."

"I'm good. But thanks," Emerson told her.

"So you're a ballerina, not a cheerleader," a voice said from behind Emerson as Chloe walked away.

Emerson turned around and saw Devane. *You knew she was going to be here,* Emerson thought. *There was no way the Divine One wasn't going to get chosen.* She forced herself to smile. She didn't want to have a thing with someone in the group. It was time for her and Devane to start over.

"Isn't it cool? We both got in!" Emerson said. "Little dogs with coats for everyone!"

Devane stared at her for a moment, then smiled. Actually smiled. "That's right. We have to start picking out cute names. Those little dogs have to have cute names."

Maybe she was more stressed about the competi-

tion than she let on, Emerson thought, happy she'd risked saying something friendly, something sort of Sophie-ish. *Maybe now that we're in the group together, everything's going to be okay.*

"I like your T-shirt." *Relax, Emerson,* she ordered herself. *You're sliding into the pathetic zone now. I like your T-shirt. Jeez.* In a second she was going to be telling Devane that she liked her socks. But Emerson really did like Brimstone127, and she didn't know the group even had T-shirts.

"It's not from the Stella McCartney collection," Devane answered, her eyes narrowing a fraction.

"That's what's cool about it." Emerson smoothed the sleeve of her Stella tracksuit self-consciously. "Brimstone127 is local. Probably only people in Miami have that T-shirt. I wish I had one. I love those guys," Emerson said.

"You *love* them?" Devane raised her eyebrows. And there it was, that attitude again, like in the locker room. "What song of theirs do you *love?*"

Emerson's brain went liquid. It was like she'd just been handed a surprise quiz in French. She loved almost all the Brimstone127 tracks. But she couldn't think of one. She glanced at the front of the classroom. Where was the teacher? Wasn't it time to get this class started? "Um . . ."

"Um," Devane repeated. She threw out her arms. "Anybody else want to give it a try? Anybody else want to try and name *one* of the Brimstone127 crew's tracks?" she called, throwing the question out to the whole room.

"'Me Against the World,'" M.J. and a massive guy answered at the same time.

"Yo, Fridge. Read my brain waves." M.J. and the guy who seemed to be called Fridge bumped fists.

"Thank you," Devane told them. She turned back to Emerson and lowered her voice. "You shouldn't try to fake that you know what you don't. It's okay, they don't teach everything at prep school."

And we're back to her hating me, Emerson thought. There had to be some way to get them back to where they could joke around again.

But Devane was already walking away.

Not good, not good, not good. Translation? Bad. Sophie was about to be late to her very first class with the Hip Hop Kidz Performance Group. *Way to make a good first impression, Soph,* she thought as she rushed out of the empty locker room—and right into ill papi.

Not just a little shoulder brush, either. A body smack. *Way to make a good first impression, Soph,* she thought again. "Sorry," she muttered.

"No prob," ill papi answered.

"Sorry," Sophie said again, her mouth taking over as usual. "But I'm gonna have to call that guy on TV. That one with the comb-over who asks, 'Have you or a loved one been in any kind of accident? Because the firm of Bad Hair and Associates and I can get you a generous settlement.'" Sophie shook her head. "Sorry to do it to you, but I need the cash."

Ill papi laughed, and that dimple of his got deeper. "I think that guy got his law degree while he was in prison."

And there it was. Yep. Sophie had just made herself another boy friend. Not to be confused with boyfriend. Not that she even wanted a boyfriend. But she wouldn't mind knowing what it felt like to have a guy look at her the way guys always looked at Sammi. Especially if the guy was as H-O-T hot as ill papi.

"You one of the new peeps in the Performance Group?" ill papi asked.

"Yep. Sophie Qian," she answered.

"Ill papi."

Sophie snorted. "Duh. Killingest dancer in the group. Son of J-Bang. I research the people I sue," she teased.

"You're whack." Ill papi got the door for her, and they were both laughing when they walked inside.

Everybody was looking at Sophie—and she knew exactly what they were thinking: What is the hottest guy in the place doing hanging with a sixth-grade non–stick figure?

Well, if they were going to look at her, she would give them something to look at. She noticed a single leg warmer by her feet and snatched it up. "Hey, my blankie!" she called. "Who found my blankie?" It was kind of weak, but it was the first thing that popped into Sophie's head.

No one answered, but a couple of the kids had started to smile. Sophie saw Emerson over to one side of the room. She hadn't even realized Em was there. Em definitely wouldn't have been sending any bad what's-he-doing-hanging-with-her thoughts Sophie's way. "Isn't it pretty, Emerson?" she called, waving the little leg warmer.

"Um, yeah, it's really lovely," Emerson answered.

"You sure that's not *your* blankie, Max?" a well-padded redheaded girl called to a much smaller girl, the smallest girl in the place. She looked like a little pixie with short, short brown hair that let you see the shape of her head.

Max the pixie laughed. "I never had a blankie. I had a giraffe named Moogoo," she answered.

"I haven't been able to sleep for days." Sophie stretched out on the floor, cuddling up with the leg warmer. "I really need a nap." She closed her eyes and gave a loud snore. Then she heard footsteps coming toward her. Someone was going to join the act? Great. But why was everyone so quiet? *We're going to change this scene so that it's less forced.*

She rolled onto her back and saw a woman in Hip Hop Kidz gear staring down at her. "I assume you're a new member of the Performance Group," the woman said.

"Yes. Yep. Uh-huh." Sophie scrambled to her feet

and used her fingers to get some loose hair back into its ponytail.

"I'm Gina Torres, your teacher." She reached over and took the leg warmer. "And this would be mine."

"Oh. Sorry. It's pretty. Have you ever considered using it as a blankie?" Sophie asked lamely.

A few kids laughed—Sophie thought ill papi was one of them—but Gina didn't even smile. She just clapped and called, "Time to get started, everyone."

Sophie sighed. *Way to make a good first impression, Soph.*

"First I want to welcome the new members of the group," Gina began. "Give a wave when I call out your name so we can start getting to know you. Ky Miggs."

"Yo!" Ky rolled the basketball he pretty much always had with him into the corner. Emerson was glad he'd made the group. It was good to see a face she knew from her old class.

"Emerson Lane." Emerson raised her hand, half expecting Gina to send her straight to Maddy's office, where she'd be kicked out for parent impersonation. Not that she'd done the impersonating herself. But close enough.

"Sophie Qian, I think you all may have seen before," Gina said. She shook her head, but a smile twitched the corners of her lips. Sophie gave a fast half bow.

"Devane Edwards," Gina continued.

"Just Devane," Devane corrected.

Emerson still didn't get what had gone wrong between them today. They'd been talking, everything had been okay, then suddenly, brrr.

"Just Devane," Gina repeated, her wild, curly brown hair bobbing around her face. "Then we have Adam and Allan Whitley."

"We're twins," they said together.

"And those are the newcomers. Welcome, welcome, welcome," Gina said. "Your teammates are ill papi, Fridge, M.J., Max, Chloe, Becca, and Rachel."

Emerson tried to memorize the names of the people she didn't know. Fridge, that was easy. Big, square fridge body. And kind of a smaller square mini-fridge head. Max was the littlest one in the group. Becca was the one with the amazing red hair. Rachel had on the Death to Pixies tee. Adam and Allan were the twins. She'd have to figure out a way to tell them apart.

"Let me do a quick rundown of the group rules," Gina continued. "It will be a good review for everybody. The rules are also in the handouts I'll be giving you at the end of class. I'll need you to have your parents sign off on them and get them back to me."

Gulp. Well, Emerson would have to forge the signatures.

She wasn't going to turn back now. She couldn't. This was where she belonged.

"First, when I walk through that door, I expect you all to be in this room and ready to work." Emerson noticed that Gina shot a look at Sophie when she said this.

"You need to dress appropriately for my class. That means athletic shoes with rubber soles. No leotards or other revealing clothing. No clothing with offensive language. No clothing promoting alcohol or any illegal substances."

As if Emerson owned any inappropriate clothing. Not with her mother.

"No food or soda in the classroom. But please, please bring in water. Plastic bottles only. And finally—this is the most important rule, so listen up—I expect teamwork. Listen to that word. Teamwork. 'Team' and 'work.' Both are important. We are a Performance *Group*, not a bunch of individuals sharing a stage. That's the team part. And the work . . . well, after today's class, you'll all know where the work part of teamwork comes in."

Gina grinned, but Emerson could tell she was serious, too. Gina definitely wasn't as casual as Randall, the basic class instructor. "Teamwork's going to be especially important next month," she concluded, then started toward the sound system. Gina looked back over her shoulder. "Isn't anyone going to ask me what's happening next month?"

"What's happening next month?" Chloe hollered back.

"Thanks for asking, Chloe." Gina turned all the way around. "Our group—our team—is going to be performing at . . . Disney World!"

The smallest girl started doing the robot across the room.

"I know it's exciting, Max. But down, girl," Gina ordered, and Max immediately stopped. Yes, Gina was tough, Emerson decided. You could tell by the way the class responded to her.

"Disney World! Woo-hoo!" Sophie cried.

Disney World, Emerson thought. *How am I going to convince my parents to let me go to Disney World—when I can't tell them why?*

"Enough talk. Let's get to work." Gina started up the music.

If that's my competition, forget about it, Devane thought, looking at Sophie as Gina led the class through a warm-up. It's not that the girl couldn't move. Devane had seen her stuff the day Maddy was making her picks, and Sophie's stuff was good. Not Devane good. But good.

Her attitude, though—it wasn't the attitude of someone who wanted to make it. Fooling around like that before class. What kind of mess was that? Her head was *not* in the game.

Whateva. Less competition was good. Yeah, the Hip Hop Kidz Performance Group was supposed to be a team and all. But they called solos *solos* for a reason. And solos were what Devane needed to get noticed. She'd seen the Hip Hop Kidz perform as many times as she could get there, and it was the kids with the solos you remembered.

Gina turned off the music. "Okay, let's start working on our routine for the Mouse. Can I get an *oh, yeah*!"

"Oh, yeah!" everyone yelled, Devane just as loud as the loudest.

"All right." Gina backed up and studied the group. "Ill papi, I want you up here on the right. Ky, you up here on the left. Chloe and M.J., middle center. And actually, Emerson, let's put you on the other side of M.J."

Devane's stomach started pumping out sour juice as she waited to hear her name. The front row and the center row were filling up. Finally Gina looked over in her direction. "Devane, you're just about perfect where you are. Just move one foot to the left."

One foot to the left. That put her in the left-hand corner of the back row. She might as well be performing in the studio when everyone else was at Disney World. No one was going to see her anyway.

You're in charge. You're the one who makes things happen, Devane told herself. *You're on schedule this far. You're in the Performance Group. You'll find a way to work it.*

Gina studied the group, moved a few people around. "Looks good. All right, we're going to start out in a wide-leg squat. Then we look left. Back to center. And shoulder rolls." Gina slowly did the moves as she called them out. Once she'd walked them through a short sequence a few times, she put on a Kanye West track.

"And five, six, seven, eight," Gina counted out. "Look left. Back. Monkey arms. Monkey arms. Slide right. Cross back. Devane, no shoulder pop on the cross. Max, the cross starts with the right foot. Right arm up, right arm out. Left arm up, left arm out. Now get ready for the flare. And drop. And swing. Devane! Legs apart. Not crossed."

Devane nodded, trying to keep her expression calm. But the cross-legged flare—that was one of her perfection moves. And the shoulder pop on that cross—it made the whole move stand out. Was Devane supposed to hold herself back just because the rest of the group couldn't keep up?

It's not my fault they don't have my skills, Devane thought. *I'm not going to dumb myself down. I'm not going to be wallpaper.*

Because being wallpaper is not part of the three-year plan.

CHaPtER 5

"I never would have imagined your sister dancing in front of an audience. And now that teacher of hers said on the phone she'll be performing at schools and malls and all over the place."

"It's not as if Sophie's exactly shy, Dad," Sammi told her father as he pulled the cab up in front of the Hip Hop Kidz dance studio. "She pretty much always says what she thinks. And she likes to joke around and everything."

Her father smiled. "True. For a while, when she was little, she wouldn't even let me get through the door without hearing a joke. 'Dad, what's the sound of someone laughing their head off?' 'Dad, why is six afraid of seven?'"

"I think it's so cool she's into hip-hop. She can be a star at school dances. And like you're always saying, it's good exercise, and—" Sammi's mouth dropped open a little. *And it's obviously a great way to meet hotties,* she silently added as she spotted her sister coming out the door with one of the—if not *the*—best-looking guys Sammi had ever seen. He had longish, dark brown hair and a great smile that turned on a dimple in one cheek. Sweet.

Sammi opened the door of the cab so Sophie could climb in. She had to get the scoop on the cutie. "So how was your first class? Did you make any new *friends*?" she asked, laying on the word *friends* so Sammi would know she'd seen her with the boy and spill.

"I got to class almost exactly when it started, so I didn't have much time to talk to people," Sophie answered. She slammed the door, and their dad pulled out onto the street. "But Emerson and Ky, these kids from my other class, got in the group, too, so that will make it extra fun. And guess what? You won't ever guess, but guess anyway."

"Ha, ha, ha, *plop*," their dad said.

"What?" Sammi and Sophie asked together.

"The sound of someone laughing their head off. Remember that one, Sophie?" their father asked.

"Yeah. That was a good one, Dad," Sophie told him. "But you're supposed to be trying to guess my news."

"Who was that you were walking out with? Is he in the Performance Group?" Sammi asked, because obviously she had to be more direct. Sophie hadn't picked up on the "friends" question.

"His name's ill papi. And yep, he's in the group. So, guesses? I'm waiting to hear guesses," Sophie prodded.

"His name can't be ill papi. Ill papi isn't a name," her

dad said.

"Okay, forget it. I'm telling. The group gets to perform at Disney World next month! Disney. World. How out in the cosmos is that?" Sophie gave a little bounce in her seat.

"That's great! Are we invited?" their father asked.

"Yeah, do we get to go?" Sammi asked, a picture of her and ill papi watching the fireworks together popping into her head, even though she'd never even said hi to the guy.

"I don't know yet," Sophie told them. "But we started working on the number we're going to do. Gina, the teacher, came up with some slammin' choreography."

"Are people in the group from schools all over the place? Like that guy ill papi—what school does he go to?" Sammi asked.

"I don't know. We didn't get into it." She turned and looked at Sammi for a long moment.

"What?" Sammi asked.

Sophie shrugged. "Nothing."

Sammi gave her little sister's arm a squeeze. "So what were you guys talking about, then? You definitely made him laugh somehow, Soph."

Sophie shrugged again. "Who knows? I'm always making people laugh, right? I just open my mouth, and it's ha, ha, ha, plop."

Their father laughed.

"See?" Sophie said.

"It's true. Everyone thinks you're funny," Sammi agreed.

"Funny, and now a Hip Hop Kid." Sophie pulled her gym bag tighter against her body.

"Yeah, Dad and I were just saying how great that is before you got in the car. And that was before we even knew about the Disney Word thing," Sammi said. *Or about the fact that you're hangin' with a guy I'd kill to get close to,* she thought.

Sophie tossed her gym bag on her bed. Disney World! She was going to perform at Disney World! "Hey, Sammi, can I borrow your Kanye West CD?" she called. She couldn't wait to try out the moves from class again.

"Yeah, come on in. It's on my dresser . . . someplace," Sammi answered from her bedroom across the hall.

"Thanks," Sophie said as she rushed into her sister's room and over to the dresser. She started rooting around, trying not to look at the cheerleading awards, and honor student certificates, and choir programs, and, and, *and* tucked into the frame around Sammi's mirror. She hated feeling jealous of Sammi. It made her feel like a big ol' troll. But sometimes when she looked at that mirror, she did.

"Here it is." Sophie pulled a CD free from the pile on the dresser. "We're using one of the tracks for our number, and I want to practice." She grinned. "Actually, I love the moves so much I just can't wait to do them again."

"So does ill papi dig Kanye?" Sammi asked.

Ill papi. *Again.*

"Here's what I know about ill papi," Sophie said. "His name is ill papi. He's in the Hip Hop Kidz Performance Group. And, um, his name is ill papi." She flipped the plastic CD case open and shut a few times. "Why do you want to know?"

The question came out with an edge. Yikes. Sophie quickly tried to cover. "You can't want to know because he's so incredibly smokin' hot, can you? You're not that shallow, are you?" she teased, tickling Sammi under the ribs on the right side, the place that always made her go into giggle spasms, no matter how mad she was. And she wasn't even mad this time. "Admit it," Sophie insisted as tears started running down her sister's face. "You must admit it."

"I admit it. I want to know because he's cute. I'm that shallow," Sammi answered breathlessly.

"You and every girl at the studio," Sophie said, stopping the tickle torture. "But I've told you all I know. Really." She started for the door. "Thanks for the CD," she said over her shoulder.

"Can I watch you practice?" Sammi asked.

Sophie tried to remember if Sammi had ever asked her something like that before. Sophie had always wanted to watch Sammi do stuff in that little-sister way. She'd wanted to watch Sammi get ready for cheerleading tryouts. Or put on makeup. Or just sing scales. But Sammi had never wanted to see Sophie do anything.

Anything like what? Sophie thought. *Did you expect her to sit next to you and watch you play Xbox?* Xbox had been pretty much Sophie's only extracurricular activity before Hip Hop Kidz.

"Sure. Let's go in the living room. There's more space," she told Sammi.

"I'll bring my CD player," Sammi said.

Sophie shoved the coffee table to one side, and Sammi got the CD player plugged in and the CD in place. "Anything else you need?"

"Nope. Just hit track three," Sophie told her. A second later the music began to thump into the room, into her body. *Look left, back, monkey arms, monkey arms,* she silently coached herself as she started the section of the routine they'd learned that day.

Sammi gave up some hand-bruising applause when Sophie finished. "You could be in a Black Eyed Peas video. You rock, Soph!"

"I could teach you some steps if you want," Sophie told her. How wild would that be? Her teaching *Sammi* something?

"I've got an even better idea," Sammi said, her dark eyes all glittery. "Can you sign up for classes at Hip Hop Kidz anytime? Or are there sessions that you have to wait and sign up for?"

Sophie felt like she'd just chugged a gallon of cold water. Her body felt chilled from the inside out. "Anytime, I think," she answered, trying to sound casual.

"I'm gonna ask Mom and Dad if I can take some classes there!" Sammi exclaimed. "My cheerleading camp is almost over. And some hip-hop moves would be great to work into some of the cheerleading routines I'll have to come up with when school starts, don't you think?"

No! Sophie wanted to shout. *No,* mhai, nein, *nope. No way, Jose, even.*

But that would not be . . . nice. And their mother wasn't the only one who thought niceness was important.

"Yeah, hip-hop is great in cheerleading. Some of the squads you were competing against last year used some locking and popping, even some breaking, and got woo-hoos from the crowd," Sophie said.

"I'm gonna go ask Dad if I can sign up for classes right away. I'm sure he'll say yes." Sammi trotted out of the room.

Sophie thought their father would say yes, too. But she wished he wouldn't.

For Sammi, Hip Hop Kidz was just one more thing. For Sophie, it was everything.

Was it so un-nice to want it all to herself?

"Eee-ooo! Eee-ooo! Eee-ooo!" Tamal shook Devane by the shoulders. "Look out. It's the fashion police. They're coming for you."

"Tamal! You made me cut this wrong! Go sit as far away from me as possible," Devane ordered, dropping the scissors.

"I'll get the tape measure," he answered. "I think the farthest away from you right now might be your bed, and you don't let me in your half of our room."

"Just go watch TV," she told him.

"You go watch TV. Go watch one of those shows where they tell you what to wear."

Devane sucked in a deep breath. It had been a hell day. She'd thought a couple of coats of her Cha-Ching Cherry, the polish she usually saved for extreme special occasions, would cheer her up. But even with her nails the fabulous deep pink, she still felt as low as she had when she left class this afternoon. Gina had pulled her aside right before she got to the door and reminded her that the Performance Group was all about teamwork, and when Devane tried to draw attention to herself by changing the choreography, she wasn't being a team player.

That's why you came up with the plan, Devane reminded herself. There was more than one way to get Gina to pay attention to Devane—and for Devane to get herself moved to the front row for the Disney World show. At the next class, Devane was going to have herself one bangin' outfit. Everyone would be looking at her. And when Gina was looking at her, she'd see that Devane was the best dancer in the room, even if Devane wasn't allowed to do her perfections like the cross-legged flare.

Best dancers got the front row. Her plan was a lock. By the end of the next class, it was front-row city for Devane. So there was no reason for her to still be feeling in the basement.

"I know ugly when I see it," Tamal said.

Yeah, every time you look in a mirror, she wanted to tell him. But her plan didn't involve getting into a battle with her brother. "Look! Tamal! It's almost time for *The Simpsons,*" she cried with mock excitement.

And he was gone. Problem solved.

Devane picked the scissors back up and started to cut. Her back-row problem was going to be solved just as easily. Uh-huh.

Everybody stared at Devane as she strolled into dance class two days later. Good. Being looked at was step one of today's plan. Slowly she walked to her spot in the back-left corner. Very slowly. So everyone could get a real good look.

Miss Emerson's blue eyes seemed like they were about to land on the floor. They'd have Ky and ill papi's eyes for company. Devane smiled at the image of all those eyeballs rolling around.

"Devane, what are you wearing?" Gina exclaimed.

Whoa. She hadn't expected Gina to say anything about the outfit in front of the whole group.

"I made it myself," Devane answered, running her hands down the tight, deep orange top. She didn't think she needed to add that she'd started with an old dress of her mama's. "It's a good color for me, don't you think?"

The shirt had a mandarin collar and short sleeves. But the real oh-yeah of it was piece she'd cut out between the neck and the top of her chest. It didn't show cleavage or anything. That wasn't the kind of attention she was going for. But the neat triangle—well, a triangle with the pointy top cut off— of skin contrasting with the orange material was poppin'.

"What I think is that you need to put on a T-shirt or a sweatshirt," Gina told her.

"Wh-what?" Devane stammered. She hadn't planned on this.

"Remember what I told all of you last class?" Gina asked the group. "We have rules about what is appropriate to wear in here. And even though I'm impressed that you made that top—I can hardly sew on a button—it's too revealing. You need to put something over it."

Devane stared at her. "I don't have anything." It was summer. In Florida. In the afternoon. Only a crazy person would be walking around with an extra shirt. Forget about a sweatshirt. People went grocery shopping in bikinis in this weather. Devane had seen them.

"I'm sorry, Devane, but you won't be able to stay in class today," Gina told her. "The rules are very important. That's why I printed them all out and sent copies home for your parents."

"I didn't know it wasn't okay. The rule sheet said no leotards. This isn't as tight as one of those," Devane protested.

"That's true, Gee. The shirt—" M.J. began.

Gina silenced him with a look. "It also said nothing too revealing," she reminded Devane. "I don't want to spend class time every week debating what is okay and what isn't." She looked from person to person as she spoke. "Some of you might have trouble making a call on what's appropriate. But I think you all know when there's no question something is okay. Just wear basic gear and you'll be fine."

She opened the classroom door. "We'll all be glad to see you next time. And it would be great if you could get in touch with one of the other kids in the group and have them go over the new moves with you."

"I'll do it!" Max called, bopping up and down on her toes. "We can meet here early. I'll teach it all to you. No problem!"

Devane shook her head. She couldn't deal with Max's extreme pep right now. She started for the door. Everyone was watching her. She felt like the door was a couple of football fields away.

"I have a sweatshirt you can borrow," Emerson called as Devane passed her.

Emerson tugged off the DKNY sweatshirt she was wearing. Underneath, she wore a plain, ordinary T-shirt that should have come from Kmart but probably came from Bloomingdale's.

"Thanks, Emerson," Gina said.

Thanks, Emerson. Thanks for coming to the rescue of Devane, who is obviously so needy, she has to make her own clothes.

Devane cringed at the thought that had slammed through her head. "No, thanks," she said loudly. "I don't need charity," she added under her breath to Emerson.

"I wasn't—" Emerson began.

"Devane, it would be a much better class if you stayed," Gina protested.

But Devane was outta there.

Like Gina really wanted her to stay. *She* was the one who decided that the top was inappropriate. It said no leotards on the rule sheet. Well, Devane wasn't wearing a leotard.

And Emerson. Why had the girl gone and gotten in Devane's business? Gina might have backed down if she knew Devane really didn't have anything else to wear. But Emerson had to jump up and down, squealing about how she had a sweatshirt.

Now Devane was going to be stuck in the back row for the rest of her life. And it was all their fault.

CHAPTER 6

Is it all my fault? Emerson wondered as she headed into the Aventura Mall. *Maybe Gina would have let Devane stay in class if I hadn't opened my mouth about the sweatshirt. Maybe Gina would have let her off with a warning about appropriate clothing if Gina knew for sure that Devane didn't have anything else she could possibly wear.*

"Maybe, maybe, maybe," Emerson muttered. She was making herself insane going over the same maybes again and again.

And she was still dealing with the issue of appropriate clothing. Not Devane's, but her own. Her mother had told her to take the car service to the mall after class and find an appropriate dress to wear to the dinner party her parents were having a week from Friday.

Appropriate. Gag. Everything Emerson owned was appropriate, down to the little tracksuits. She totally loved those wild purple-and-orange camouflage pants that Sophie had and the goofy Happy Little Puppy T-shirt Chloe was wearing in class today. And she'd almost drooled over that top Devane had made. But her mother would have vetoed all three of those. She probably would have burned Devane's top!

Emerson couldn't fight the veto. Which didn't put her in the shopping mood. She decided to hit L'Occitane first. Her mom had asked her to pick up some linen water. Lavender Harvest. Largest size. Pour top, not spray. She found it quickly and paid.

She wished her mother had just told her exactly what dress to buy, too. It's not like Emerson's opinion mattered, and it would be easier knowing what her mother was expecting her to come home with instead of going through all those racks trying to guess. Emerson usually called it right. But she'd had to make a few returns.

Now for the next unnecessary purchase. Emerson hesitated outside L'Occitane. Should she go to Saks or Macy's to look for the acceptable but pointless dress?

Saks, she decided. It was closer. And it was near the place with the yummy cookies. She took two steps in that direction and blinked. Olivia Pitre was coming toward her. "Olivia!" Emerson exclaimed. "You're not supposed to be here!"

"Should I go away?" Olivia teased when she reached Emerson.

"That's not what I meant. I just meant, shouldn't you still

be at the Jamison Intensive?" Emerson asked.

"I am," Olivia told her. "I'm only back until Saturday. My mom's fiftieth birthday is tomorrow, and my dad's giving her a surprise party. I'm part of the surprise. I'm staying at the Biltmore tonight so I won't be spotted."

"So what am I missing out on at the Intensive? Tell me everything!"

"Everything?" Olivia smiled. "Where to start? There are classes, classes, and more classes. All kinds of ballet. Pointe. *Pas de deux*. Character. Some modern dance and jazz, too. And stuff like nutrition and dance history. It's incredible. Just to do this one thing you love all day, every day. I can't wait for the *Nutcracker* auditions this year. My dancing has gotten so much better already. And this year you know we're moving up to snowflakes."

Emerson felt oily guilt slide through her body. Sometime she was going to have to tell her parents the truth about ballet. She was going to have to tell them that she'd made an executive decision to veto it and the *Nutcracker*. She shoved the thought away. It was summer. She didn't have to deal with the snowflake issue right this second.

"Now you have to talk," Olivia rushed on. "You have to tell me all about everybody in ballet class. I want to know all. Like I heard that Felicia broke up with Jared. Can you believe it? They've practically been going out since kindergarten!"

"Um, I don't really know," Emerson admitted.

"How's that possible?" Olivia asked. "You're in class with her every week."

"I don't know. I take the class. There's no talking in class. I leave." Emerson shrugged. "I guess you're the one I mostly talked to." Except she hadn't talked to Olivia all summer. Or written her.

It hadn't occurred to Emerson that she'd fallen out of touch with her ballet friends. *When did that start?* she wondered. Probably ever since she'd been feeling that ballet wasn't as important to her as it always had been. "I've been doing something new this summer," Emerson told Olivia. "I've gotten really into hip-hop. I'm in a Performance Group and everything."

"No way! We did a little tiny bit of hip-hop at the Intensive," Olivia answered. "But how are you going to perform with them and do the *Nutcracker*?"

Is the Nutcracker *all anyone cares about?* Emerson thought. "I think . . . I think I'm going to pass on the *Nutcracker* this year," she admitted.

Olivia's eyes widened. "No way! That's our big chance. We get to perform with professionals. At the Intensive they say that's really important. That it's never too early to start making contacts."

Emerson tried to think of something else to ask Olivia about. Something not related to dancing of any kind. But she couldn't come up with anything. "I guess I should go. My mom has ordered me to buy a dress." *Is it completely obvious I just want to get away from Olivia?* Emerson wondered. She shifted her L'Occitane bag to the other hand. "Want to come with me? To Saks?" she added quickly.

"That's okay. I've, um, got to go to the bookstore. To buy my mom a present," Olivia said. It kind of sounded like she was lying. It kind of felt like Olivia was ready to get rid of Emerson, too.

Emerson was relieved. She didn't know what she and Olivia would talk about if they kept hanging together. "Okay, well, see ya when you get back."

"Yeah, see ya. But I might get moved up one level in the fall." Olivia gave a half wave, then turned and walked away.

I can't believe the only thing we had to talk about was ballet. If I'm not interested in ballet, Olivia has no interest at all in me, Emerson thought. *I wonder if we'll be friends at all when she gets back.*

And it's not like Emerson had made any new friends lately. Devane's face rose up in front of her. Friends, no. Enemies . . . maybe.

"My sister taught me some moves. We're the kind of sisters who are friends, too. Not the kind that fight all the time," Sammi told Maddy Caulder. Maddy was subbing for Randall, the regular teacher of the basic hip-hop class. Sammi hadn't even met Randall yet. Today was day one for her.

Maddy shook her head. "I still can't believe it's your first class. You're picking up everything so fast."

"I guess cheerleading helps, too. We're always learning routines," Sammi told her.

"Okay, guys, let's go through it once more. People on the left, watch me. People on the right, watch Sammi. Remember, we're all doing the same moves. We're just doing them in opposite directions."

In the mirror Sammi saw the kids behind her nod and smile. "All right," Maddy said. "And five, six, seven, eight. Step out. Shoulder up. Shoulder out. Head out. Knees in. Knees out—toes out."

Maddy continued to shout out the moves, and Sammi followed along, snapping her arms and legs and shoulders and neck in the series of motions. It made her body feel juiced, like there was this electric current running through her veins. No wonder Sophie loved this stuff!

"Foot behind and turn," Ms. Caulder concluded. She turned around and applauded the class. They applauded back. "Very nice. Randall will be back next week. He'll add on to the combo, and you'll start working it to music."

Sammi grabbed her sweatshirt off the floor and used it to wipe down her neck and face. She pulled the rubber band out of her hair and let it fall loose in a black stream down her back. Did she have time to run to the locker room for a quick coat of lip gloss?

No, she decided. Sophie's Performance Group class was supposed to start up in the room down the hall in ten minutes. Sammi didn't know how early ill papi liked to get there, so she couldn't risk being in the locker room when it was the right moment to just *happen* to run into him.

"Thanks for helping me out with that last part, Sammi," Maddy said as Sammi headed out the door. "It makes it easier if there's someone up in front demonstrating each direction."

"It was fun," Sammi told her. Then she took a deep breath and stepped out in the hall. A quick glance in both directions showed that ill papi wasn't around yet. She uncapped her sports bottle and drained the water that was left.

Sammi wasn't too worried about what to say. With boys, it didn't really matter. Just talking to them at all— looking at them, maybe a fast arm touch—showed you were interested. And that was pretty much that.

A flash of movement near the boys' locker room caught her attention. Uh-huh. There he was. Sammi headed down the hall, timing her walk so that she'd intercept him before he reached the door of his practice room.

"Hey, you're ill papi, right?" she asked when she was close enough. She gave her hair one quick flick. The hair flick was a really effective boy-attention grabber. But Sammi reminded herself not to use it again in this conversation. Too much flicking could make a girl look nervous. Or like she had a scalp condition. Eww.

Ill papi's eyes followed the hair flick. But he didn't move closer. *Hmmm.*

"My sister's in the Performance Group with you. Sophie."

Ill papi nodded. That was all. *Hmmm.*

"And I just started taking classes today because the stuff you do in the group is so killer."

He nodded again. And backed up a step.

Backed up. As in away from her. Sammi's brows came together.

No boy had ever stepped *away* from her before.

"Look at that." Sophie took a step closer to the window.

Emerson stopped her pre-class stretching and moved over next to Sophie. She looked through the practice room window and into the hallway. "What am I seeing?"

"You are seeing something that no one has ever seen before," Sophie said, using her best TV infomercial announcer voice. Then she realized she was attracting a little attention from the other people waiting for class to start, so she continued more softly, a lot more softly. "You're seeing my sister crash and burn with a boy. Ill papi, to be exact about it."

"Your sister's taking classes here?" Emerson asked.

Well, since she's standing there all sweaty in a tracksuit, that would be a yes, Sophie felt like saying. But Emerson didn't deserve her snark.

"Yep. She's in our old class. Oh, he's looking at his watch," Sophie said. After the watch check, ill papi took a step away from Sammi. Big I-don't-want-to-be-talkin'-to-you cues. Sammi said something else, then gave it up and retreated. Ill papi headed for the drinking fountain without as much as a backward glance at Sophie's sister.

Unsuccessful. Sammi hadn't even gotten a smile out of him. Unbelievable.

"At least she's brave enough to make the attempt," Emerson said. "I'm one of those girls who's gone to, like, one school dance. And I stood by the bleachers, paralyzed. If a guy had tried to talk to me, I'd probably have said something like, 'Um, me?' And actually approach one—nuh-uh."

Sophie laughed. "I'm pretty much the same."

Emerson wagged her finger at Sophie. "Liar. You talk to boys all the time. I've seen you. You've talked to every guy in this class. M.J. Fridge. Ky. The twins. And ill papi. They all love you."

"I talk to them. But I don't *talk* to them."

"You're gonna have to explain," Emerson told her.

"I talk to them, but it's not guy-girl talking," Sophie said. "Because of the fact that they don't even realize I'm a girl. They don't think I'm a male, exactly. They don't think about it either way. I'm just a buddy."

"So, you talk to them all the time. I never talk to them. But we're both basically chickens around them," Emerson summed up.

"I wouldn't say I'm a chicken," Sophie protested.

"But if there was a guy who did see you as a girl . . ." Emerson said.

"Okay. Yeah, it would feel a lot different. It would be hard to talk to him. I don't think I'd be able to joke around the way I usually do," Sophie agreed.

"Hey, we're having a conversation. Not about dance!" Emerson exclaimed.

"Yeah. So?"

"So, nothing." Emerson bent down to tie her shoelace, even though it was already tied.

"So?" Sophie asked, bending down to tie her own lace, even though it was also already tied.

"So, I don't know, I was just thinking it was kind of like maybe we were becoming friends," Emerson said in a rush, her face close to Sophie's. "How dorky is it that I said that out loud?"

Sophie grinned. "Very dorky, my friend, very dorky."

She straightened up and saw ill papi stride into the

room. She winked at Emerson and rushed over to him, then whipped the baseball cap off his head. She hugged it tight. Then held it out in front of her and stared at it, frowning.

"Sorry, I thought it was my teddy bear," she told ill papi.

He laughed. *Sammi couldn't do that,* Sophie told herself. *She couldn't even make him smile.*

Immediately Sophie felt bad for having such a mean little thought. She tossed the hat back to ill papi. "Better keep it on. You don't want people to see your bald spot."

Ill papi laughed again, then his smile kind of slid off his face, and he took a step closer to her. "Can I ask you something, Soph?"

Her heart started doing a stutter move in her chest. Was he actually going to *talk to her* talk to her?

"I just wanted to know . . ." He hesitated. "Your sister, what grade is she in?"

"Ninth. She's three years older than me," Sophie answered, on autopilot.

Ill papi nodded and walked off. Sophie stared after him.

Wha-huh? What was going on? Out in the hall, ill papi looked like couldn't wait to get away from Sammi.

But just now . . . just now he'd acted the same as every other boy who'd come up to Sophie to score info on Sammi.

That would mean—hold on. Stop right there. Red light.

Did ill papi like her sister?

"I like my little spot all the way in the back, in the corner," Devane told herself as she headed into the practice room. It wasn't true. But she told it to herself anyway, because she wanted to be a gold-star student today. Getting known as a troublemaker was not part of the plan.

"Hey, everybody," Gina called. "I want to get started. But I have an announcement first. We have a new performance scheduled over at Gulliver Academy next Friday. That's one of the magnet schools for the performing arts. The show will be a month before the Disney World show, so it will be a great chance for us to make sure we have all the kinks out."

"Yay!" Max started leaping around like a cheerleader. The girl had as much energy as Tamal after a family-size box of Froot Loops.

"I know you love the idea of being onstage, Max," Gina told her, "but get it under control. Or you and I will have to step outside for a chat."

Max got herself under control. Why did Gina have to go all drill sergeant? Max was just a little excited.

Devane actually was, too. So a high school wasn't the place to get discovered. So she'd be dancing in the back row. She'd still be performing, with all those lights on her. She couldn't wait.

"We've got a lot of work to do. Today we'll finish up learning our new number. I want to assign some solos for a couple of places. Our new members also need to start learning our old routines," Gina said.

Devane's brain froze on "solos." A plan B had just opened up in front of her. No, she was down to plan C already. A sizzlin' plan C. Scoring a solo would be just as good as getting herself into the front row. Better. She focused on Gina, listening for what she had to do to be picked.

"Ill papi and M.J., I want you to kick it off," Gina continued. "You'll come out from opposite sides of the stage. I have a little piece worked out for you. Then everybody will enter."

So it was a done deal. Plan C was a dud before it had even started up. Gina had already made her choices. "Chloe and Sophie, I want you each to turn around and break out on your own for a couple of moves after that section where everyone is facing toward the back—where we ended up last time. We'll go over the steps later."

New kids were getting solo time. Maybe Devane would, too.

"Then right before the end, we're going to do an add-on. Emerson's going to start us off. Then Devane will come in. Then Max. Then Becca. Then we'll reverse it. Becca will go out. Then Max. Then Devane. And Emerson will finish us off. We'll work on that at the end of next class." Gina looked around. "Any questions?"

Yeah, Devane wanted to say. *How'd you decide Blondie gets to be the one owning the spotlight at the start and finish?*

How it killed Devane not to say it.

CHAPTER 7

Emerson sat in front of one of the mirrors at the long table in the Gulliver Academy dressing room. This school obviously went all out for its theater department.

As she carefully put on her eyeliner, she reviewed the finish of the add-on, the part where she was alone again. Gina had heard from Maddy about the way she'd seen Emerson incorporating ballet into her moves, and Gina had decided to have Emerson do some of those moves solo at the end of the sequence.

"You ready to get it done, ballerina?" Devane asked, dropping into the empty chair next to Emerson. *Why'd Sophie need to go to the bathroom right now?* Emerson thought. That chair should have been occupied. She so didn't need to deal with the Divine One right now.

"Sure, I'm ready. A little nervous. But I always am before a show, and I think it keeps my focus sharp," Emerson answered. "What about you?"

"Me? I'm all good," Devane answered. She leaned

toward the mirror and used a tissue to flick away a tiny clump in her mascara. "Hip-hop's in my blood."

Was Devane trying to psych her out? Emerson searched the other girl's face, trying to figure out her deal. "I've been dancing onstage since I was five. And that was with a professional ballet company," she finally answered.

Brag much, Emerson? she thought. *It's not like you were chosen to be a mouse in the* Nutcracker *because you were some kind of phenom. When you're five and you're playing a mouse, you're mostly supposed to be cute. And what five-year-old in a mouse costume isn't cute?*

"Ooh. A professional ballet company." Devane widened her eyes in mock admiration. "Did Mumsey and Daddy buy one for you?"

Don't just sit here and take this, Emerson ordered herself. *Just because she's talking doesn't mean you have to listen. You have legs. Walk away.*

Emerson stood. "I've got to go warm up," she said.

Devane stood in the wings, ready for her first moment onstage. Her very first.

Unlike Miss Em-er-son.

The audience applauded as the music came pounding out and M.J. and ill papi started things up. The two guys owned the crowd. Devane could feel the excitement coming off all those people. M.J. and ill papi were creating that.

I could do that, too, she thought. *I could make those people feel something. But not from the back row, left-hand corner.*

She needed to be patient. The calendar on her wall at home covered a whole year for a reason. Her plan for world domination took three years for a reason. Big goals took big time. For now, what Devane needed to do was be a good little back-row Hip Hop Kid. Gina had to figure out eventually that Devane deserved a solo.

Okay, count it off, Devane thought. *And five, six, seven, eight.* She swung herself out onto the stage, making sure to smile big at Gina on her way past and smile even bigger for the audience—whichever of them could see Devane. Then she launched into the routine, giving the moves everything but without adding any extras.

Now, left foot behind and turn. Devane stood facing the back wall. She heard a burst of applause. That would be for Chloe doing her thang. Another burst. That would be for Sophie doing her solo moves. How must it feel to listen to that clapping and cheering and know it was just for you, all of it?

Devane wasn't going to find out. Not today. She spun around with the rest of the class. Swing kick left. Swing kick left. Elbow out. Fist up. The dance moved so fast. Devane wasn't nearly ready for it to be over, but Emerson was already moving front and center for her solo. Getting her applause.

Why does she get front-and-center time? Devane thought for the millionth time. She shoved the thought away. She needed to concentrate. She was almost up. She counted the beats, and there it was—her cue.

Devane broke out from the back of the group and joined Emerson. They flashed through their moves, some in sync, some in opposition. The crowd gave it up for her, too. Her and Emerson. Devane tried to tell herself that more of it was for her. But there was no way to know. Because this wasn't a solo.

Then here came little Max. They all dropped low, doing some eggbeaters and slides, then using a kip up to get back on their feet just as Becca joined them, her red hair flying. More applause. For all of them. It felt good. But it would have felt better if Devane was sure it was for her.

Look left. Follow your head around. Keep it low. Low is funky. Pump the arms, opposite hip action. Gina's voice pounded through Devane's head. But she didn't need to hear it anymore. Her body had this mastered. She owned this.

Becca moved out. Devane worked the moves. Right elbow up. Right fist up. Left elbow up. Left fist down. Switch it. She couldn't see the audience. The lights were too bright. But she could hear them. And she could *feel* them. Max moved out. The crowd was sending out that same charge they'd been pumping to M.J. and ill papi.

But this time all that energy was coming straight at Devane and Emerson.

And in a few more beats Emerson would have it all to herself again. Devane wasn't ready to give it up. Why should she? She was as good a dancer as Emerson. Forget that. She was better.

Devane flashed on watching Sophie and Emerson that day Maddy had been observing the classes to choose new people for the Performance Group. Emerson had been goofing around, doing some ballet moves hip-hop style— almost like what she'd be doing for her solo at the end of the sequence. And Sophie had been clowning up the moves and tossing them back to her. Everyone had loved it. Maddy had loved it. Devane could still see the smile on her face.

This crowd would love something like that, too. So when it was time for Devane to go out, she didn't leave.

Emerson launched right into her first solo move with no hesitation. Devane could tell she was a little freaked, but that was only 'cause Devane was up close. Wouldn't matter as long as Emerson kept going.

Devane crossed her arms and leaned way back and watched Emerson, the way Sophie had done. Then after a couple of beats, she launched into the pirouette Emerson was locking through but doing it up Devane style.

The crowd hooted and hollered. And it was for Devane. All for Devane.

Emerson got what Devane was doing, and she reacted just the way she had with Sophie. Getting into it, playful battle style. The crowd took it up a notch, loving the way Emerson gave it right back to Devane.

They picked up the pace of the battle. And the audience went frantic. They were lovin' the show. When Devane and Emerson slammed to a stop, some people actually jumped to their feet. Their feet.

The applause was still ringing in Devane's ears when she and Emerson rejoined the rest of the group and fell in with the steps of the finale.

People don't give it up like that for wallpaper.

Emerson kept the smile on her face until she was completely offstage and she was sure that no one in the audience could see her. Then she dropped it.

"Are you okay, Em?" Sophie called, rushing up to her. "I can't believe Devane did that!"

"I can," Emerson said. "That is so totally, completely like her. All she cares about is herself!"

"That was so tight, what you did out there," she heard M.J. say. She glanced over her shoulder. And yes, he was talking to Devane.

"Did you hear that? M.J. thinks it was fabulous," Emerson exclaimed. "And Devane looks like she just won an

MTV award for best video or something."

"No one in the house knew anything was wrong. That's something," Sophie said, patting Emerson gently on the arm. "Although I should take Devane to task for stealing my moves. She took her whole part of the routine from me!"

"You'll have to wait in line," Emerson answered, surprising herself. "I'm going over there and kicking her behind. Well, in a talking kind of way."

She didn't wait to hear what Sophie would say. She was afraid if she waited, she wouldn't do it. And if she didn't do it—she'd never be able to look at herself in the mirror again without wanting to vomit.

Emerson strode straight over to Devane. M.J., Max, Becca, and Fridge were clustered around her. *Congratulating* her. Not Emerson's problem. She wasn't going to wait to talk to Devane in private. Everyone could hear this. She wanted them to.

"You said you weren't a diva the first day I met you. You lied!" she exclaimed.

"What's this mess you're talking?" Devane asked, raising one eyebrow.

"I thought you were just having fun, little dogs and your stretch SUVs and your movie-star boyfriends," Emerson rushed on. "But you really are a diva. Divas only care about themselves. They expect everyone else to do everything they want because they are so, so special. Well, that's you,

Devane. And you want to know another word for diva? Selfish!"

"Hold up!" Fridge protested.

"You're calling *me* selfish?" Devane cried, looking at the people gathered around with a *can-you-believe-this-girl* expression. "You're just mad because you didn't get every single second alone in the spotlight that you think you deserve."

"Come on, you guys," Max said. "Don't fight. We just had a great show."

"It isn't about the spotlight," Emerson insisted, ignoring Max. She felt angry tears sting her eyes, but she blinked them away. The very last thing she wanted was to let Devane see her cry. "What you did was completely unprofessional. We rehearsed the routine a million times. Why? So we could do a great performance."

"That's right," she heard someone say softly. She wasn't sure who. Her eyes were locked on Devane.

"And you just bust in there, break all the rules because *you're* mad you didn't get a single second alone in the spot-light!" Emerson rushed on.

"In case you didn't notice, I gave a great performance," Devane shot back. "Those people out there loved me. They weren't disappointed they didn't get to see your perfect practiced, practiced, practiced routine. Did you hear that applause they gave up for me?"

"I heard." M.J. moved a little closer to Devane.

"That applause was for both of us," Emerson snapped. "Because I held it together and—"

But she found herself talking to Devane's back. Devane was already walking away.

"Uh-oh," Max said softly.

Emerson followed Max's gaze—and saw Maddy and Gina. Oh, no. What had they seen? How much had they heard? They hadn't been there when she'd launched into her attack on Devane, Emerson knew that much.

Could this day get any worse?

CHAPTER 8

Devane stepped into the lobby of the Gulliver Academy auditorium, and it was like she was back onstage. All that energy pouring into her. All her little cells had to be glowing. Her heart was doing some hip-hop of its own inside her chest. She didn't care what the ballerina said. Devane had rocked the stage, and it was the most sizzlin' experience of her life.

"How long have you been taking lessons?" a tall guy called to her. "You were awesome."

"I was born awesome," Devane called back with a wink.

"That duet you did with the blond girl was so funny," a girl wearing a pale blue sweater set told Devane. "But it looked really hard. Did you two have to practice a ton?"

Devane shook her head. "Well, the other girl had to practice a lot. But not me." She'd meant it to sound like a joke, but the words came out with more bite than she'd intended.

"Will you sign my program?" the girl asked. "I want to have your autograph when you're a star. 'Cause I can tell you're gonna be one."

Getting asked for an autograph wasn't on Devane's calendar until next year! "Of course." She took the girl's Hip Hop Kidz program and signed it the way she'd always planned. *Follow your own light. XXOO. Devane.*

"Thanks!" The girl disappeared into the crowd. Devane looked around. Maybe somebody else wanted a Devane signature. She wondered if anyone would ask Blondie for hers. She didn't see Emerson around anywhere. But she did see Gina and Maddy heading toward her.

Devane waved at them. She couldn't wait to hear what they thought of the spin she'd added to the ballet combination. They had to have seen the way the crowd grooved on it.

It was so killer that Maddy was in the audience today. Maybe she would decide to invite Devane into the Professional Group right away. That group was one step above the Performance Group. They got some insane gigs. Not that Disney World was nothing. But the Professional Group did slammin' performances all the time. They'd even been in a Lil' Krypto video. A video! Getting in the Professional Group now could knock a year off Devane's schedule.

"We need to talk to you. Come backstage, please," Gina said when she and Maddy reached Devane.

Yeah. They want to talk to me in private. They don't want audience people hearing Hip Hop Kidz business. Like who gets invited to be in what group, Devane thought as she followed Gina around to the backstage area. It had pretty much cleared out.

"I can't believe what I saw from you during the show," Gina burst out.

"Thank—"

"What you did showed no respect for me. It showed no respect for the team," Gina rushed on. "It was complete diva behavior."

Devane felt like she'd been slapped. "Everyone loved it. Didn't you hear them? I got the most applause of anyone."

"We talked about teamwork the very first day you were in my class, remember?" Gina asked. "Devane, it's clear I can't trust you. I can't send you out onstage not knowing what you're going to do. You could have ruined the entire show with that little improv. Your behavior might have thrown everyone else off. Did you even think of that?"

"But it didn't," Devane said.

"That's because Emerson saved you. She covered for you."

"I knew she'd get what I was doing. I saw her and Sophie doing almost the same thing once." Devane turned to Maddy. "Remember? That day you were watching their class."

"I remember," Maddy answered. "But Devane, Gina's right. Everyone in the Performance Group has to be a team player. I'm sorry, but we're going to have to put you on probation."

A wave of dizziness swept through Devane. "What?" That was the only word she could get out. She closed her eyes, trying to concentrate, then opened them. "But I'm the best dancer. Maybe M.J. is better than me. But I'm the best girl."

"You're a phenomenal dancer, Devane. But talent isn't all that it takes to perform with a crew," Gina answered. "You'll be able to keep coming to class. But no performing until further notice."

No performing? Why not just tell me no breathing? Devane thought. She felt her eyes begin to burn, and she ordered herself not to cry.

She crossed her arms over her chest. Gina and Maddy needed her. And they knew it. "No," she told them.

"I beg your pardon?" Gina said.

"No. No probation. I won't stay in the group if I'm on probation," Devane told Gina and Maddy.

Maddy raised her eyebrows. "Then you aren't giving me any choice, Devane. You won't be able to stay in Hip Hop Kidz."

Sammi spotted Sophie and ill papi halfway across the lobby. Ill papi was looking at Sophie and laughing. Sophie could always make guys laugh. Guys and everyone else.

She rushed over to Sophie and gave her a hug. "You were fab up there. I was telling everyone you're my little sister."

Impulsively she turned toward ill papi. She was going to give him a hug, too. It wouldn't seem too strange. She'd just hugged Sophie to say congrats. And the theater people at her school were always hugging each other all the time. "You were amazing, too."

Ill papi tensed up as soon as her arms went around him. What was with the guy? He'd seemed all relaxed and cool when he was talking to Sophie a minute ago. Did he not like Sammi for some reason? She let him go and took a step away. She needed to be the one to step away first.

"Is that the same show you're going to be doing at Disney World?" she asked, looking mostly at Sophie, although she did a low-level hair flip in ill papi's direction. She thought he noticed it, but she wasn't sure.

"Part of it," Sophie answered.

"I gotta go," ill papi said. "There's a bus in fifteen."

"Our dad's going to swing by and pick us up in his cab," Sammi told him. "I'm sure he could drop you off."

"It's no big. See you, Soph." And there he went. All, "See you, Soph." Like there was no Sammi.

Sammi stared after him. She didn't get it. It's like she'd become the "before" in a deodorant commercial or something. And it was sort of like Sophie was the "after." At least ill papi didn't run screaming every time Sammi's sister was around. The way he did with Sammi.

"What were you and ill papi talking about when I came up?" she asked.

"I don't even remember," Sophie said. "What did you think of my solo?"

"Supah-fly," Sammi answered. "That combo that started with the side kick—it ruled. Even more than the four hundred times I saw it at home." She knocked shoulders with her sister. "So what were you guys talking about? You had the boy practically giggling like a little girl."

Sophie rolled her eyes. "Oh, yeah. I was asking him how he got the name ill papi. I was asking if was because he broke the record for projectile vomiting."

"You did not!" Sammi fake-shrieked.

"You know me. I'll ask anything." Sophie shrugged.

The way to get to ill papi couldn't be by talking about puke. Sammi would not accept that.

"Hey, here comes Maddy," Sophie said. "I hope she liked the show."

"There's no way she didn't," Sammi answered.

"Hi, there, Qian girls," Ms. Caulder said when she came to a stop in front of them. "Sophie, I just wanted to say what a great job I thought you did in your very first show. I'm so glad you agreed to be part of the Performance Group."

"You're glad? I'm the one who's glad. Ecstatic, thrilled, overjoyed . . . I can't even think of enough words," Sophie told her. She smiled so big, Sammi thought she might crack her face open. She couldn't remember the last time she'd seen Sophie so happy.

"Good to hear it. And I think your sister might be just as talented." Maddy turned to Sammi. "It looks like we're going to have an opening in the Performance Group much sooner than I thought. I'm not going to make any decisions about filling it right now. But after seeing you in class the other day, I have to say, I'm thinking about you as a possibility."

"Really?" Sammi couldn't believe this. How cool would it be to get all *TRL* onstage? How cool would it be to be able to see ill papi a lot more?

"Really," Maddy answered. "The Performance Group class is right after the class you're taking now. Feel free to sit in if you want to. Check it out."

"That would be the best!" Sammi looped her arms around Sophie's shoulders. "The Qian girls together!"

Sophie smiled at her. Her mouth muscles must have gotten tired, Sammi thought. Because it wasn't the crack-her-face grin Sophie'd had on before.

Emerson headed through the lobby, her gym bag over her shoulder. She'd already changed out of her costume and washed off her stage makeup. She'd gone straight back to the dressing room after her showdown with Devane. There was no one she'd needed to see right after the show.

Not like Sophie, she thought as she spotted Sophie with her arm around her older sister as they chatted with Maddy.

Emerson's mother had gone to every single ballet recital Emerson had ever had. She lived for them. Emerson wondered if her mother would have come to the show today. If Emerson hadn't needed a French tutor. And if there had been a way for Emerson to do hip-hop and ballet— including the *Nutcracker*—without damaging her GPA. And if Emerson hadn't had to lie just to be here today.

"Your duet was amazing," a tall guy told Emerson as she reached the door.

"Thanks," Emerson said, not bothering to mention that her duet was supposed to have been a solo.

"Can I get an autograph?" the guy asked.

"Really?" Emerson asked.

He nodded. "I already got your partner's."

My partner. Right, Emerson thought. "Sure," she said. The guy held out his program and pointed to a spot right next to Devane's lavish one-name-only signature. Her own name looked too neat and prim when she added it.

"Cool. Thanks," the guy said.

"Thank *you*," Emerson said. "That was my first auto-graph ever." *And giving it should have been a lot more fun,* she thought.

She stepped out into the hall and headed for the main exit. The car would be waiting for her. She hoped Vincent was driving. She could use somebody to talk to about the Devane madness. Their fight kept replaying in her head. And she thought the only way to get it to stop looping was to talk it out. Vincent would be the perfect—

"I'm talking to you!"

The loud voice cut into Emerson's thoughts. She turned around and saw Devane. Perfect. Just what she needed, another confrontation with the Diva.

"Why didn't you stop before?" Devane demanded.

"I didn't hear you," Emerson said. "I was thinking. You should try it sometime."

"Yeah, you can make jokes now that you went running to Mama." Devane took a step closer, getting up in Emerson's face.

"What?"

"What?" Devane repeated. "Don't act all innocent. I know you went crying to Gina and Maddy about how wrong it was for me to steal your solo."

Emerson shook her head. "Devane, I didn't say anything to them. But it turned out they heard part of that fight we had. I don't know how much."

"So it's just the same as if you went running to them," Devane shot back. "They heard you wailing about how I stole some of your spotlight. About how I was so selfish because I didn't let you have it all to yourself. You—"

"Devane, stop," Emerson ordered, surprising herself. "Gina and Maddy didn't need to hear me say anything. They didn't need me to tell them that what you did was wrong. Everybody in the group knew it was wrong. And Gina definitely didn't need me to tell her you changed the choreography. Did you think she wouldn't notice?"

"Everybody did *not* think it was wrong," Devane insisted, her eyes hot.

Emerson remembered M.J. telling Devane how tight he thought her moves were. "Okay, not everybody. But if Gina and Maddy did, they came up with it on their own. They don't need me to think for them."

"So you're telling me you think I'd still be out of the group if they didn't know how upset I'd made precious little Em-er-son?" Devane demanded.

Wait. Emerson's mouth opened, but she couldn't think of what to say. She had mush head again. Why did that keep happening to her around Devane?

"Yeah, you can't deny it's all your fault," Devane accused. "Or that you're happy about it. It's exactly what you wanted. Now you won't have to deal with me anymore."

"I didn't—" Emerson started to protest. "I'm not—"

But she was talking to Devane's back. Devane was already rushing away. That kept happening.

CHAPTER 9

Emerson slid on her very appropriate dress, zipped it up, and made sure she hadn't mussed her French braid. There was a light tap on her door. A half a second later, the door swung open, and her mother stepped inside. Her mother always did that—knocked, then came in without waiting for an answer.

"You look lovely, sweetie-poo," she told Emerson.

At the use of the pet name, Emerson felt something crack inside her. She suddenly wanted to hurl herself at her mom like she was a five-year-old again and sob out the whole story of her horrible, hideous, humiliating day. How Devane had almost ruined the performance. And how Devane had yelled at her. And most of all, how Devane had tried to blame Emerson for Devane's getting kicked out of the group. Even though Emerson had nothing to do with it. At all.

But that would mean telling her mother what a big, fat liar Emerson was. And that's all they'd end up talking about. How wrong it was to lie. And how disappointed her mom—

and her dad, because he'd have to be told, of course—were in her. And how she'd ruined her life and her college career by quitting ballet. And how now her mother wouldn't get her picture in the paper. Well, that wasn't true. Her mother was *always* getting her picture in the paper for some charity thing. But how now her mother would get her picture in the paper one less time.

And then Emerson's parents would strap her into a pair of toe shoes and she'd never, ever get to do hip-hop again.

"You aren't getting sick, are you?" Emerson's mother asked, pressing her hand against Emerson's forehead.

"No. No, I'm fine," Emerson said quickly. "Why?"

"You just looked pale to me is all," her mother answered. "Our guests should be coming soon. We should be downstairs to greet them."

Emerson's phone rang. Her mother nodded, giving Emerson permission to answer it.

"Hey, I just wanted to make sure you were okay after the ruckus," a voice began after Emerson said "hello."

"Sophie?"

"Of course. So are you okay?" Sophie asked.

Emerson glanced at her mother. Her mom was looking through Emerson's jewelry box, probably searching for the most appropriate necklace. "So you heard about Devane . . . not coming to class anymore?"

"What?" Sophie exploded. "No! Tell!"

"She said she was out. And it was my fault." Emerson shot another look at her mom. She didn't seem to be listening.

"I need a lot of details," Sophie said.

"I can't right now. My parents are giving a dinner party, and I need to be there," Emerson answered.

"Okay, second reason I called. My own loving parents want to take me and my sister out to celebrate the show and—well, I'll fill you in on the other part later. I want you to come with us. Movies tomorrow. We can pick you up."

"One sec." Emerson put down the phone. "Mom, one of my friends from, um, dance wants to know if I can go out to the movies with her and her family tomorrow."

"Which girl?" her mother asked.

"You don't know her. She's new," Emerson said. "Her name's Sophie Qian. Her parents will pick me up."

"Sounds fine." Her mother held up a simple gold chain. "Wear this. It will be perfect with this dress. And don't be long."

"Okay," Emerson said as her mom left the room. She picked up the phone. "Sorry I made you wait. My mom says I can go."

"Yay! Let me write down your address."

Emerson rattled off the address, hearing the doorbell ring downstairs. "I have to go let my parents show me off to their friends."

"Fine, but you're telling me every single word Devane said tomorrow. We'll pick you up at one." Sophie hung up without saying goodbye.

Emerson smiled. She felt like it was the first time she'd smiled in about a week. Then she sucked in a deep breath and headed out of her bedroom and down to the party.

Her stomach started attempting a flare in her belly when she saw Mrs. Hahn in the front hall. Mrs. Hahn, as in the mother of Bailey Hahn. Bailey Hahn, as in one of the girls Emerson had been in ballet with since forever.

Mrs. Hahn was one of those moms who not only went to every recital, but stayed to watch every *class*. So she knew Emerson's secret. At least half of it. She knew Emerson wasn't going to ballet anymore.

"Emmy!" Mrs. Hahn cried. She rushed over and kissed Emerson on the cheek. "It's been too long. Haven't you been feeling well?"

Emerson's mother turned toward them at the question. And Emerson's stomach started trying to do what felt like cross-legged flares. Not that a stomach had legs. But that's still how it felt.

This was it. Emerson's life was going to end right now.

"I thought she looked pale myself," Emerson's mother said. "But she said she's feeling fine, so fingers crossed."

The doorbell rang. Emerson's mother started toward it. Emerson's father asked Mrs. Hahn a question about her golf game.

And the crisis was over.

For now.

But how long until all my lies come out? Emerson thought.

"So Devane said she was out of the group because Gina and Maddy knew you were upset about what she did?" Sophie demanded.

"Yeah." Emerson flopped down on the padded plastic seat of the bench next to the row of sinks in the movie theater ladies' room. And Emerson wasn't much of a flopper. She was a proper sitter-downer. Sometimes she even crossed her ankles.

Sophie snorted. "That's such bull—baloney. Like Maddy and Gina wouldn't have minded that she changed the choreography if you hadn't gotten upset about it."

"That's what I told Devane! I told her they'd still be mad even if they hadn't overheard me saying anything to her." Emerson sighed. "So why do I feel so bad?" She shook her head. "Right after the show, I was furious. But now, when I think of Devane being kicked out of the group, I just feel kind of sick to my stomach."

"It's because you're way too nice," Sophie told her. "Or because you're way too stupid. You haven't actually started believing that trash Devane spewed, have you?"

"No. Not really. I just—" Emerson shoved herself off the bench. "You know what? We aren't going to talk about this anymore today. This is supposed to be a celebration of you getting in the Hip Hop Kidz Performance Group and our first show and everything. I'm not going to ruin it talking about Devane."

"It's also a celebration of Sammi practically getting into the Performance Group," Sophie reminded her.

"It is pretty amazing that Maddy asked her to sit in on the Performance Group class when Sammi's only been taking the basic class for about a week," Emerson said.

"Amazing. Yeah. That's our Sammi. She does eight amazing things before breakfast." Sophie rested her head against the cool plaster wall. "Wow, that came out bitter, didn't it?"

Emerson shrugged. Which in polite Emerson-speak meant, "Yeah, it came out really bitter, Soph."

"You want to know a secret?" Sophie asked.

"Yeah. I do. I really do," Emerson said. "You know mine already. You know my parents have no clue I'm even in the Performance Group."

"Okay. I'm going to sound like a troll person, but I'm jealous of my sister. There it is. It's out there. A big puddle of stink. See, Sammi's good at everything. She's a cheerleader, but she's not just a cheerleader—she's head cheerleader.

She's a great student, but she's not just a great student—she's on the honor roll. Fill in about fifty more examples and you've got my older sister."

Emerson nodded. "Sounds kind of hard to live with. I don't have any brothers or sisters. All I have to compare myself to is the perfect Emerson my parents think I could be if I tried a little harder," Emerson said. "The one who speaks French like a Parisian. And who definitely doesn't do hip-hop."

"I deal with most of the Sammi stuff okay," Sophie said. "I'm proud of her, even. And most of the time she's my best friend. But I just really, really wish she hadn't decided to make Hip Hop Kidz one of her things, you know?" Sophie concluded. "It's totally selfish, but I wanted it to be just mine."

"It's not so selfish to want one thing of your own," Emerson said. "I want it, too. I want it so much, I don't care how my parents feel. I don't care that I have to lie to them pretty much every day."

The door swung open and Sammi poked her head into the bathroom. "Come on, you guys, the movie's about to start! You're missing the celebration!"

"We'll be right there," Sophie said. She looked over at Emerson. "Can I get a woo-hoo?"

Emerson pumped her fist in the air and slapped a big grin on her face. "Woo-hoo!"

Sophie had always thought her sister was her best friend. But she was starting to realize that wasn't true anymore. Emerson was the person she wanted to tell her secrets to and complain to and just have fun with.

"Do you think Maddy will make an announcement about Devane before class or what?" Emerson asked Sophie as they sat in the locker room before class.

"She'll have to say something," Sophie answered. "She can't just—"

The door swung open, and Sophie stopped speaking.

"Talking about Devane?" Chloe asked, dropping her gym bag on the bench across from them.

"Do you have radical bat ears or what?" Sophie asked.

"I don't think bats have better hearing than people. They do that echolocation thing. But that's different," Chloe answered. She started taking earrings out of the multiple piercings in her right ear. "I just figured you were talking about Devane because you looked so hush-hush."

"What have you heard?" Emerson asked, her face wrinkled up in a worried expression.

Poor Em, Sophie thought. *She clearly still has that sick feeling she told me about over the weekend.*

"That she got probation because she was such a complete diva at the show," Chloe answered.

"Probation?" The word came out of Emerson's mouth in a squeak.

"Wait! Probation!" Sophie echoed. "I heard she was out."

"She is. Devane supposedly got all huffy about the punishment and quit. M.J.'s about to explode," Chloe told her.

"Well, that was pretty dumb of her. She should have just taken the probation," Sophie said.

Chloe shook her head. "That's not why M.J. was mad. He didn't think Devane deserved probation in the first place."

Emerson made a small adjustment to one of her socks. "Do you?"

Sophie wanted to hear this. She couldn't believe even one person in the group was okay with what Devane had done. But maybe M.J. just thought probation was too harsh.

Chloe shrugged. "Gina is all about respect and rules. And what Devane did—that was like smacking her in the face. You don't just trash Gina's choreography without a world of pain coming down on you. That's almost like breaking all the rules at once." Chloe started de-earringing the other ear. "I mean, why am I sitting here pulling all this stuff out of my ears? Because Gina says only one pair at a time in class."

"I'm still freaking. It might not look like I'm freaking. But I'm freaking," Sophie said. "So Devane just basically told Maddy and Gina to shove it?" *Leaving a spot open that*

Sammi might be able to take? the smelly little troll voice asked.

Chloe raised her eyebrows, which seemed to remind her that she had a little gold loop in the right one. "You sound surprised. Devane isn't exactly the kind of girl who thinks she should be told what to do," she said as she pulled the loop free. "Be back in a minute. I have to take a whiz." She covered her mouth and smiled through her fingers at Emerson. "I mean, use the facilities."

"Does everyone think I'm a complete priss or something?" Emerson cried when Chloe had disappeared into the bathroom. "Like they can't even say 'whiz' in front of me or I'll have a conniption?" She threw up her hands in exasperation.

"Jeez, calm down. I think you might actually have raised your voice," Sophie said.

"See, even you think it," Emerson accused.

"You want me to say 'whiz' in front of you? I'll say it instead of 'hi' from now on," Sophie promised.

Emerson let out a sigh that sounded like it came from the bottom of her feet. "No, it's just . . ." She took another look around the locker room. They were still alone. "Do you think everyone thinks I'm a total rule-follower? They all heard me yell at Devane for changing the choreography and cutting in on my solo. What if they think like Devane? What if they think Gina and Maddy only put Devane on probation because I made a fuss because I'm such a priss?" Emerson rubbed her face with her fingers.

"You're not a priss because you got on Devane for shoving herself into your solo. Pretty much anyone in the group would have wanted to kick her tail for that. I would have for sure," Sophie told her. "Devane just wants someone to blame for what happened. You saved her bacon out there. She should have been kissing your feet after the show. Each and every little piggy," she added, trying to make Emerson laugh. It didn't work. "Just because covering for her onstage wasn't enough to keep her from getting probation—that's not your fault." Sophie hoped some of this was sinking into Emerson's noggin. "And it's definitely not your fault that the Diva had a temper tantrum and quit."

Max burst into the locker room. "Devane's out!" she exclaimed. "Devane's out of the group!" Her voice became higher with every word.

"We were just talking about that," Sophie told her.

Max put on an exaggerated pout. "I wanted to be the one to tell." She started stepping up and down on one of the benches like she was in step class. Not that Sophie had ever been in step class. But she'd seen a few while she was channel surfing. Before hip-hop, channel surfing was her main form of exercise.

The locker room door opened again and Sammi hurried in, followed by a few sweaty girls who were probably in her basic class and Becca from the Performance Group. The basic class kids were usually changing out of their dance clothes while the kids in the Performance Group were using the locker room to get ready for class. "I'm serious," Sammi was saying to the girls. "No detail is too small."

"I saw him drinking a Yoo-Hoo once." Becca laughed as she unzipped her backpack and pulled out her sneakers. "You're telling me that detail isn't too small?"

Emerson raised her eyebrows at Sophie, asking a silent question. Sophie shrugged. She had no idea what her sister was talking about.

"Nope," Sammi said. "That's one point for Becca. Remember, whoever gets the most points wins a fabulous prize." Sammi opened her locker. "Whoever gets the most points wins—" She rummaged around inside the locker. "Wins this fabulous *People* magazine that is only two weeks old." Sammi held up the magazine and riffled the pages.

"What do you have to do to get points?" Max asked, dropping to a seat on the bench.

"One fact about ill papi equals one point," Sammi answered with a grin.

The troll in Sophie's head started to stomp around. So Sammi hadn't given up. Clearly she was determined to get ill papi interested in her. And when Sammi was determined to get something—watch out. She'd do whatever it took. That's why she was the best at everything she did.

Sophie shot a glance at her sister. *You're gonna get a spot in my Performance Group any day now,* she thought. *Do you really, really need to get the hottest guy in the group, too?*

Of course it's going to take a little more effort to get noticed by the hottest guy in the place, Sammi thought. *He's used to having tons of girls pay attention to him.* She stood in front of the bathroom mirror, trying to get in game head for another "accidental" encounter with ill papi.

You look great, she told herself as she blotted her lipstick on a rough brown paper towel. *And you've studied for the test. You've done your research.*

Well, this is a first—you're giving yourself a pep talk before meeting a guy, Sammi thought as she shook her head at her reflection, then turned and hurried out of the bathroom, through the locker room, and into the hallway. She'd spent so much time prepping, she had to find ill papi fast or the Performance Group class would start before she got a word out.

Oh, score. There he was. Over by the soda machine. She could go over and complain to him about how it was always out of Yoo-Hoos. But that didn't seem like exactly the right thing to bond over.

She couldn't believe she was putting this much thought

into what to say. She'd never had to plan like this with any other boy. But ill papi was a special case.

Sammi ran through the facts she'd learned about him. It wasn't a long list. That ill papi, he was sort of a boy of mystery. She knew he drank Yoo-Hoo. He liked those Madden NFL PlayStation games. He had an *Aqua Teen Hunger Force* sticker on his backpack. Max had seen him pet one of those little black-and-white dogs with the big ears one time.

And that was it.

Yoo-Hoo is a risky opener, Sammi thought as she walked toward ill papi. She could imagine the convo. Her: *I love Yoo-Hoo. They should have Yoo-Hoo in this machine.* Him: *Yeah.* Then nothing.

Sammi had never played Madden NFL, but she did know football. She'd cheered for a ton of games, and she knew exactly what went down on the field. But how to bring the whole thing up? Her: *You might not know this, but I'm a cheerleader and I love football. Do you perhaps love football, maybe of the video game variety?* Him: *Let me get your sister. You seem to be having some kind of brain malfunction.*

There was no more time for strategy. She was two feet away from him. It was now or never. Sammi pretended to study the soda available in the machine. "I saw that *Aqua Teen* sticker on your backpack the other day. I love that show," she said.

Actually, Sophie loved that show. But Sammi had half

watched it while Sophie was watching it. It was about a hamburger, some french fries, and a Coke—she thought it was a Coke—fighting crime. Or solving mysteries. Or something.

"It's pretty funny," ill papi answered. Then he walked off.

Without even looking at her.

"Becca was looking at me funny in the locker room. I think she thinks that it's my fault Devane's out," Emerson told Sophie as they headed to class. Emerson hesitated outside the door. She wasn't ready to go in there. "How many other people do you think blame me?"

"I told you. No one is going to think it's your fault. Becca was probably looking at you weird—if she even was—because she's trying to figure out how it's possible for a human to get her hair into such a perfect French braid. She probably wants to know if there's a special device you use but is feeling embarrassed to ask."

Emerson laughed. She couldn't help it. There was something about Sophie. No matter how bad you were feeling, she could make you feel better . . . just by being Sophie.

"Now come on." Sophie took her by the arm. "Others need to see the braid. Don't deny them." She tugged Emerson into the practice room.

Max, Chloe, M.J., and Fridge were already inside. And all

of them were staring at Emerson. At least that's how it felt. But maybe she was overreacting. Maybe they'd glanced over at her the way you glance at anyone who enters a room. Just to see who it is.

But the thing was, glances and stares last a different amount of time. And M.J. and Max were definitely staring now. "Hi," Emerson said, feeling her face heat up. She had one of those faces that really showed a blush, too. She hated that.

"Hey," Chloe answered with a smile. She stepped forward in a lunge and pressed the heel of her back leg down, stretching out her calf muscle.

"*She* clearly hates you," Sophie joked softly. Then she gave Emerson's arm a squeeze and released her.

M.J., Fridge, and Max hadn't said anything. But it's not like a quiet little "hi" required some big response. Or any response.

Gina usually had the class work on the Kanye West number after warm-up, so Emerson headed to her opening position on one side of M.J. As she looked at him, Chloe's words went through her mind.

M.J.'s about to explode.

Doesn't mean he blames me, Emerson thought.

She cleared her throat, then made herself speak. "Hey, M.J., I can't wait to do the Kanye number at Disney World, can you?"

He turned and stared at her. Full-on, no-mistake stared at her. And didn't say anything. She'd asked him a question. She hadn't just spit out a little "hi" that someone could answer or not answer.

O-kay. M.J. was dissing her. And it could only be about Devane.

"Em," Sophie called from across the room. "I saw this cool combo on *TRL* last night and I'm trying to break it down. Help me?"

"Sure," Emerson answered. *Thank you, thank you, thank you,* she added silently to Sophie. She lifted her chin, squared her shoulders, and headed over.

The twins came in as Sophie started showing Emerson the steps. They were talking to each other, ignoring Emerson and everybody else, but that was normal.

"Why is it so quiet in here?" Ky asked when he entered. No one answered. He shrugged. Bounced his basketball a few times, then stashed it in the corner.

He doesn't seem mad at me, Emerson thought. She wished she could just focus on the moves she and Sophie were working on instead of trying to put everybody who came through the door into either the friend or enemy camp. Make that enemy or not-enemy camp. Right now Sophie was the only one who really felt like a friend.

Ill papi came in, followed by Sammi a few moments later. Neither looked especially happy. But neither paid any attention to Emerson.

Then Gina entered, and the whole group came to attention. "I have an announcement," Gina said.

Here it comes, Emerson thought, trying to brace herself.

"Well, two of them, actually," Gina continued. "I'm pleased to announce that Sammi Qian will be sitting in on our classes. She's a talented dancer, and Maddy and I think she's someone who might be a great part of the Performance Group somewhere down the road. Everyone give her a big welcome."

There was some applause, but not much. Emerson felt bad for Sammi. The lack of enthusiasm didn't have anything to do with her. It's just that everyone knew Sammi had been brought in as a replacement for Devane.

Gina used her fingers to push her curly hair away from her face. "Second, I'm sorry to say that Devane will no longer be with our group."

"Sorry, right," Emerson heard someone mutter. She thought it was Fridge.

"Does someone have something to say?" Gina asked, her voice crisp and cool, her eyes narrowed on Fridge. Clearly Gina thought he'd been the speaker, too.

Max raised her hand. "Go ahead," Gina told her.

"Why?" Max asked.

Gina hesitated a moment. "Maddy and I had decided to put Devane on probation for changing the choreography at the Gulliver Academy show," she answered. "That was unacceptable to her, so she chose to leave Hip Hop Kidz."

"Why?" Max said again.

Gina frowned. "I don't know what you're asking."

"Why was she going to get probation?" Max burst out.

"I've just explained it. She changed the choreography. She could have ruined the performance for all of you," Gina said, color rising to her cheeks.

"All of us?" a girl—Emerson was almost positive it was Becca—said very softly. "Don't you mean *one*?"

"You still think no one believes it's my fault that Devane got kicked out?" Emerson whispered to Sophie.

CHAPTER 10

"Hey, Sammi!" ill papi called as they left class.

He knows my name, Sammi thought. *And he's using it. Nice.*

She turned around with a mid-level hair flip. "What's up?" she asked, with another hair flip. *Too much,* she told herself. *He's gonna think you have dandruff.*

"I just wanted to ask you what the name of the hamburger in *Aqua Teen* is," he said, pulling a notebook and a pen out of his pocket.

"Um . . ." Sammi thought frantically, trying to remember *any* names she'd heard during *any* of those Adult Swim cartoons Sophie watched.

"EEEE!" A buzzer sound came out of ill papi's mouth. Loud and harsh and inhuman. "Wrong. There *is* no hamburger. There's a meatball. Are you telling me you don't know the difference between a hamburger and a meatball?"

"I'm a vegetarian," Sammi sputtered. She flipped her hair again, and again, and again. White flakes fell like snow onto her shoulders, piled up, then drifted softly to the floor and settled at her feet in dandruff drifts.

"EEEE!" Ill papi gave that ear-burning sound again. "Then why did you say you drink Yoo-Hoo? Yoo-Hoo is made of liver and brains! EEEE! EEEE! EEEE!"

"Sammi, are you ever going to shut off your alarm clock?" Sophie yelled from the next room.

EEEE! EEEE! EEEE! EEEE!

Sammi sat up and slapped her alarm clock. It tumbled to the floor and went silent. *What a horrible dream,* she thought. *What a monster of a horrible dream.* Her encounter with ill papi a couple of days ago before class hadn't been great. But at least it hadn't been anywhere near that bad.

She rolled out of bed and hurried into the living room. It was Saturday, but she definitely didn't want to go back to sleep. She didn't want to risk falling into that dream again. "Thanks for waking me up," she told Sophie. Her sister was practicing the combo Gina had showed them right at the end of class. "You pulled me out of this gruesome dream."

Sophie didn't ask for details. And Sophie loved to hear about dreams, anybody's dreams.

"I can't believe you're up before me," Sammi commented. "You're the original bed slug."

"I wanted to get this down." Sophie turned the music up a little and got back to working the moves.

Sammi studied her sister. She didn't looked flushed or

pale or anything. But there was something off about her.

"I could use some practice, too." Sammi got in sync with Sophie. For about three seconds. Then Sophie stopped.

"I'm gonna hit the shower. If you go first, you'll use all the hot water." She snapped off the music—even though Sammi was still dancing—and started out of the room. "Don't eat all the Froot Loops," she called back.

Even though Sophie knew Sammi hated that cereal.

What is with her? Sophie thought. *It's like she's mad at me. But I haven't done anything.*

Emerson moved front and center for her solo. She checked the classroom mirror to make sure she was in position, then launched into her pirouette. Her body went through the locking she'd rehearsed so many times. But Emerson felt . . . nothing.

She definitely wasn't the full-out Emerson today. She was going-through-the-motions Emerson. She'd been that way all class. Gina had called her on it a few times, and Emerson had tried to force herself out of the dull grayness that seemed to be surrounding her, pushing her down. But she couldn't.

Doing these same moves at the Gulliver Academy show had been exhilarating. It was as if the air had had double the amount of oxygen. Or as if gravity didn't have its usual pull.

There was this energy zapping back and forth between her and the audience. And between her and Devane.

Distracted by the thought, Emerson came out of the pirouette a beat early. "Concentrate!" Gina called out.

Emerson tried. But there was energy zapping around today, too. Bad energy. Lightning bolts that stung every time Becca or M.J. or Max or Fridge looked her way. This was the second class without Devane. How many classes would be like this?

She moved into the steps of the finale, then the number was finally done. And so was class. All Emerson wanted to do was get home. It used to be that all she wanted to do was get *here*.

"You definitely look like you could use pizza," Sophie said as they headed toward the locker room. "Let's change quick and get over there."

"Over where?" Emerson asked.

"No one told . . ." Sophie let her words trail off. "Unbelievable."

"What?" Emerson demanded.

"I was probably supposed to tell you," Sophie said. "We're going to meet up at that pizza place on the corner."

"We? Who's we?" Emerson asked, already knowing the answer but hoping she was wrong.

"The group. Sorry. I don't know where my brain is." Sophie whacked herself on the forehead. "I was supposed to ask you, I'm sure."

Emerson stopped walking, forcing Sophie to stop, too. "You weren't supposed to ask me."

"Well, Max was actually organizing it. But she probably thought because we were friends that I—"

"Give it up," Emerson said. "We both know it's not true. But thanks for trying."

Sophie linked her arm through Emerson's. "You're going," she said.

"There is absolutely no way," Emerson answered. Even thinking about it made her feel hot and itchy with humiliation. She wasn't showing up where no one wanted her.

"You can't let them bully you out of the group," Sophie insisted.

"I won't. This isn't the group. It's pizza," Emerson told her. "I'll be here for the next class. And the next one. And the next one."

Even if I hate every single second.

Sammi took a careful bite of veggie pizza—she didn't want that thing to happen where a string of cheese connects the slice to the mouth—and studied ill papi. He was chatting away to Rachel about some alternative band that Sammi had never heard of.

Maybe when she went home, she should go online and

research the band and—no. She'd just end up with a repeat of that *Aqua Teen* sticker fiasco. She needed something else. Something different. Something bold.

And until she came up with whatever it was, she needed to just act like a normal human being. She tried to focus all her attention on the conversation going on around the table. ". . . the competitions," M.J. was in the middle of saying. "Last year we had some fierce ones. I was thinking there were ones we lost that we might be able to win with Devane in the group."

Her eyes drifted over to ill papi. *What is my problem?* she thought. It's not like she hadn't been around cute guys before. They'd never turned her inside out like this.

And some of those cute guys . . . they had liked Sammi. A lot.

"But there are lots of great dancers in the group," Sammi said, mostly to get her brain off ill papi for one single minute. "I mean, you're amazing, M.J. Don't you think the Hip Hop Kidz group can take down those other crews even without Devane?"

"A couple of solos from the right dancers make a massive difference," Becca said. "You saw Devane at the show. She lit up the audience. I even saw a couple of people asking her for her autograph afterward."

"We need Devane," M.J. stated firmly. "And even if we didn't, what went down with her wasn't right."

"Are we here to have pizza? Or are we here to talk about Devane?" Chloe complained.

"What do you have against her?" Max snapped.

"Nothing. But we have other things to talk about. Like Disney World. We should come up with a plan," Chloe answered. "Which rides to hit, in what order and all that. It's a big place, and there are long lines for a lot of stuff."

"Space Mountain," ill papi said.

Great, Sammi thought. *He likes roller coasters. And they make me want to heave.*

"No." Ky shook his head. "That one with the water. What's it called? It's the—"

"We're not done talking about Devane," Fridge interrupted. "We haven't decided what to do."

"We can't do anything. Get real," Chloe said. "Devane quit. End of story."

"But she might want to come back if a certain person wasn't in the group anymore," M.J. said.

"A person named Emerson," Max agreed.

Sammi sat up a little straighter. They were talking about the girl who was, like, her sister's best friend in the group. Sometimes Sammi felt like Sophie liked Emerson more than she did her own sister! Sophie hadn't come to the pizza place because no one had asked Emerson.

"Right. Let's bump her off," Ky joked, rolling his eyes.

"All we have to do is keep on with what we're doing,"

Fridge said. "She's not going to keep showing up if she knows no one wants her around."

You haven't done anything wrong, Emerson told herself as she hesitated in front of the rehearsal room. *Just get in there.*

She couldn't believe it was already time for class again. It felt like it had only been a day since the last nightmare, not a week. And Sophie had given her the heads-up that M.J. and company were going to keep on freezing her out.

Let them, she thought. She'd already lied to her parents to be here. She wasn't going to let a few kids force her to leave. She sucked in a deep breath. If only her plan had worked out. She'd wanted to get settled in the classroom before anyone else got there. Somehow she'd felt like that would give her an advantage. But through the window, she could see that Max, M.J., and Fridge were already inside.

Emerson forced herself to open the door. She could feel the stares, like those laser beams they used for surgery. If eye-shaped holes had appeared in her skin, she wouldn't have been surprised.

"Hi," she said from the doorway. She wasn't going to slink in there like a criminal. No one answered. But just speaking had made her feel slightly better. After all, you should never enter a room without acknowledging the others present. Her mother had taught her that.

Emerson strolled over to her usual spot and began doing some stretches. Her muscles were tight with tension. Her lungs felt a third of their normal size. She couldn't get in a deep breath. This was making her crazy.

"It's not my fault!" Emerson burst out suddenly, her voice echoing in the mostly empty room. "I know you think it is. But all I did was tell Devane off for busting in on my solo. That's it. I didn't know Maddy and Gina were listening. I wanted Devane to hear me. I didn't care who else did. Because that's how mad I was."

Sophie and Chloe slammed through the door. "Hey," Sophie said, breathless. "We heard there was a party goin' on. My invite must have gotten lost in the mail."

You deserve so much more than a thank-you note, Sophie, Emerson thought. *Even a thank-you note with a home spa gift basket like the ones Mom always sends to the women on her committees wouldn't do it.*

"Your friend got Devane kicked from the group," M.J. told Sophie. "Are you okay with that?"

"Devane quit." Sophie said each word slowly and carefully, like she was talking to a preschool kid.

"Only because she got slapped with probation—after Emerson threw a hissy," Max said.

Chloe rolled her eyes. "You all know Gina. How can you be surprised she wanted Devane on probation after what she did? She dragged you out in the hall and lectured you for five minutes for drinking 7-Up in class, remember, Fridge? She wants every rule followed."

Fridge nodded. "She said if I wasn't willing to follow all the Hip Hop Kidz rules, I shouldn't be there. Said if she saw me doing it again, I'd have to go home."

Muscles in Emerson's back and shoulders began to relax a little.

"Devane said—" M.J. began.

Sophie didn't let him continue. "Devane thinks Devane is perfect. Devane's head would melt and run down her neck if she had to accept that she'd actually done something stupid."

"What are we playing this time?" ill papi asked, joining the group gathered around Emerson. She wished they'd all take one giant step back. She'd even be willing to say, "Mother may I?"

"Who Wants to Be a Millionaire?" Sophie told him. "The question is: Why is Devane no longer in our group? A: Emerson told Gina and Maddy to put her on probation and they do everything Emerson says. Because this was so unfair, Devane quit. B: Gina and Maddy wanted to make the group a little worse, so they decided to put one of the best dancers on probation just for fun. Because this was so wrong, Devane quit. C: Devane pulled a diva at the show, and Maddy and Gina—all by themselves—decided she deserved proba-

tion. Devane pulled another diva and quit when they told her. D: Devane was actually a secret agent and her mission was over."

"This isn't a joke," M.J. muttered.

"Yeah, it is," Sophie shot back. "It's a joke to think there's anybody to blame for Devane not being in the group but Devane."

How does she always know what to say? Emerson wondered. Sophie never seemed to get mush brain.

"She *did* pretty much do it to herself," ill papi agreed. "She didn't have to quit. Maybe we should just tell her we want her to come back—just suck up the probation and come back."

Chloe shook her head. "You think Maddy and Gina are just going to let her prance back in here like that?"

"She'd probably have to—" Adam began.

"Apologize big time," Allan finished for his twin.

"Do we even want her back?" Chloe asked. "If she'd hijacked my solo . . ." She shrugged.

"She's the best dancer we've ever had in this group," M.J. insisted.

"Best *girl* dancer," ill papi corrected.

"Yeah," M.J. agreed. "We need Devane if we want to win more competitions this year."

"But if she was going to try and come back, she would have done it by now," Chloe said.

That made sense to Emerson, but she didn't chime in. She felt like *she* was still on probation.

"Like I said, we need to tell her we want her back," ill papi said.

"And that she has to apologize," Rachel added.

"*If* we want her back," Sophie told him. "Here come Ky and Becca. We should vote or something. If people want her back, we come up with a plan to get a person who thinks she's incapable of error to apologize. And you know Gina and Maddy will know if she's not sincere."

Chloe glanced at the clock. "If we're doing this, we gotta do it quick. Gina's going to be here in a few."

"Get over here, you guys," M.J. called to Ky and Becca. "We're taking a group vote. Do we want Devane back in the group or not?" He shot a glance at Sophie. "Like it takes a vote. So who thinks we need to get back someone who's one of the best dancers we have?"

M.J., Max, and Fridge instantly raised their hands. Ky, Becca, and ill papi raised their hands a moment later. Then Adam, Allan, and Rachel. Emerson raised her hand, too.

"Are you mental?" Sophie demanded.

"I don't have a problem with her being in the group," Emerson said. People had falsely believed she'd been responsible for Devane getting kicked out. She wasn't going to actually be responsible for keeping her out now.

"I don't care if she comes back as long as she doesn't

screw up again," Chloe said.

"She didn't," M.J. protested. "She made the show better. The two of them"—he nodded at Emerson—"tore up the place."

Emerson blinked. She couldn't believe those words had come out of M.J.'s mouth.

"Because Emerson didn't panic when Devane decided to be a hog," Sophie said. "Devane could have ruined the show." She shrugged. "But if Emerson's willing to give her a second chance, I am, too."

"Okay, then. M.J., you should talk to her," ill papi said.

"I think Emerson should do it," Becca suggested.

"What?" Emerson and half the rest of the group cried.

"Look, if Emerson tells Devane that everyone wants her back, Devane will have to believe it because Emerson is the person who has the most reason to want Devane to stay gone." Becca used both hands to shove her long red hair away from her face.

"She's right. You do it," M.J. told Emerson.

The muscles in her shoulders and back—the ones that had been getting looser and looser—all tightened back up. So did muscles in her neck and jaw. So did muscles in places she didn't even know she had muscles.

"Devane hates me," Emerson protested. "She's not going to want to hear anything I have to say."

"What Becca said makes sense to me." Ky gave the

basketball he still held a bounce.

Emerson glanced at Sophie. "They could be right," Sophie told her. "But that doesn't mean you should do it."

"No, I will." This was a team. And she was a team player. Even if Devane wasn't. "But I don't know where she lives or anything."

The door opened and closed. Gina? Emerson jerked her head to the entrance. No. Sammi.

"Am I missing something important?" Sammi asked.

"Nothing you need to know about," Sophie said. "I can tell you later if you want."

"Gina always brings the class list with her." Max shifted her weight from foot to foot as she spoke.

"So someone needs to distract her while Emerson gets a look at it," Ky said.

Everyone—including Emerson—immediately turned to Sophie.

"You think you could do something to get yourself yanked out of class for a lecture?" Chloe asked.

Sophie laughed. "I guess I could come up with *something*. Right near the end of class, okay? All of you get into whatever it is I do. That will draw the wrath of Gina."

"Sophie is excellent at drawing the wrath." Sammi put an affectionate arm around her sister's shoulders.

"I'll help you look through Gina's stuff," Ky told Emerson.

Going through a teacher's stuff behind her back.

Emerson's mother would be so proud. Emerson couldn't help smiling a little at the thought.

"Thanks, Ky." The words were barely out of her mouth when the door swung open and Gina came in. The group scattered. Gina gave them all a long I-know-something's-up look, but since she couldn't figure out what, she started the warm-up.

Emerson tried to keep her focus on the dancing, but her eyes kept wandering to the clock. She needed to be ready when Sophie did . . . whatever it was Sophie was going to do. Emerson would have only one chance to get Devane's address. And if she got caught, she was sure she'd end up on probation herself.

Here it comes, she thought about five minutes before class ended when Sophie stopped cold in the middle of a routine and raised her hand.

"This better be good, Sophie," Gina said.

"I have something to confess," Sophie began. "It's something I've been doing. Something that's not fair to the team."

"What?" ill papi demanded, already getting into the scenario.

"I've been foot synching," Sophie told him, blinking rapidly, like she was trying not to cry.

"So-phie," Gina warned.

"No, it's wrong. It's something no real dancer should do. I've just been footing the moves, not actually doing them,"

Sophie continued.

"Like lip synching for feet!" Chloe burst out. "That's an insult to all dancers."

"Sophie should be kicked out!" Max exclaimed.

"Enough!" Gina cried. "For the last time, I want quiet, and I want it now."

The noise in the room stopped almost instantly. "Sophie, we've talked about your comedy routines before," Gina scolded. "Not in the classroom. They waste time. And we need every moment to get ready for our performances." Her eyes swept over the group. "That goes for the rest of you. You act like you've decided to become an improv group. If I see this again, maybe that's what you can do with yourselves. But you won't be in my class, I can tell you that. Now please remove yourselves."

"It's just that I needed to cleanse my sole about the foot synching," Sophie insisted. "Get it? S-o-l-e."

Gina closed her eyes and sighed. "I want to talk to you outside, Sophie," she finally said. Then she opened her eyes and led the way to the door.

You're awesome, Soph, Emerson thought as Gina and her friend stepped into the hallway. There was only one problem. Gina was standing facing the window. Which meant that she had a full view of the classroom as she talked to Sophie.

Emerson and Ky exchanged a worried look. Was the plan going down in flames?

Can I just grab Gina by the shoulders and turn her around? Sophie wondered.

No, that would be just too psycho. Sophie was willing to help with the whole get-our-diva-back plan—especially because Emerson was down with it. But Sophie wasn't willing to get put on probation herself. Or get taken away from the dance studio by the men in white coats.

"I'm having trouble understanding, Sophie," Gina continued. "I stood right in front of you and told you to quit messing around and you wouldn't let it go."

Sophie got an idea. She bit down on the inside of her cheek—hard. Hard enough to get some tears going. "I'm sorry, Gina. Sometimes when I've got everyone laughing and everything, it's hard to stop." She brushed her hand across her eyes, trying to draw Gina's attention to the tears, and gave a tiny sniffle. She didn't want to blow it by being too dramatic. "Sorry," she said again, and turned away from Gina.

Come on, Gina. Come on, Sophie thought.

A moment later she felt Gina's hand on her shoulder. Now Sophie and Gina were both facing away from the window into the classroom.

You better go for it now, guys!

Ky caught Emerson's eye, and they quietly moved to the front of the class. Gina had the class info in a folder stuck behind the CD player. Ky slid it free, and they stood shoulder to shoulder, studying it.

Emerson kept shooting glances at the window. Yeah, Sophie still had Gina facing away.

"Right there," Ky said.

Emerson whispered Devane's address a few times until she thought she had it down. Then she nodded to Ky, and they blended back into the group. Just in time. Gina opened the door a second later. "That's all we have time for today. See you next week. All dance, no comedy. Got me?"

She got a bunch of yeses and nods in reply. Emerson hurried out into the hall and over to Sophie. "Sorry you had to get in trouble. Was it horrible?"

"No worries. Gina just talked—loud and a lot," Sophie answered as they headed to the locker room. "We needed a team effort. And I'm the goofy one on the team."

It had felt good doing something as a team. Especially after feeling like half the people in the group were against her.

But Emerson wouldn't have the team with her when she faced Devane. She was on her own now.

Devane usually loved being on her own in the apartment. No Tamal to pluck her nerves. But today it felt too quiet.

She flipped on the TV. Three different judges on three different channels telling fools how big of fools they were. Dr. Phil saying, *"What are you thinkin'?"* Cartoons. Shopping. She turned the TV off. None of that was going to hold her attention.

What Devane needed to do was take herself into her room and rework her calendar. Hip Hop Kidz wasn't the only way to cash, cars, and world domination. She just needed to figure out a new plan, rework the timetable a little. Maybe she could even find a faster way to the top.

Except that Disney World show really would have helped.

"Get your behind off this couch, get in there, and do what has to be done," she said out loud, talking to herself like she was Tamal. She responded the way Tamal would, too. She slunk deeper into the couch and turned the TV back on.

She'd just started getting the rundown on a case about two bad neighbors and one bad dog when the doorbell rang. Probably one of Tamal's friends looking for him. Devane stood up, walked over to the door, and peered through the peephole.

Huh-uh. She was not seeing what she was seeing. The ballerina stood out there. In Devane's hallway. Where Ms. Hackie had left her cat's full litter box. Nasty.

Devane didn't want Emerson in her apartment. Devane and her mother had watched a million decorating shows and done as much as they could to fix it up. But it was still one tiny place for three people. Devane's mom didn't even have a bedroom. She had to fold out the couch every night and sleep on it.

The doorbell rang again. The girl wasn't giving up. And Devane really didn't want her spending more time in the hall. With that thin, curling wallpaper that always reminded Devane of skin that was just about to peel off.

"I guess you want to come in," Devane said as she pulled open the door. She stepped back so Emerson could pass her. "Have you instructed your chauffeur to come to your rescue if you're not downstairs in five minutes? You know Overtown is dangerous. You hear about it every night on the news, am I right?"

Emerson sat down on the couch, looked Devane in the eye, and said, "Everyone in the group wants you to come back." She cleared her throat.

"Well, that's too bad. I quit that mess," Devane said. *I knew it,* she thought. *I knew they needed me.*

Emerson shook her head. "You've got so many stories. You told me you were out. You tried to make me think you got *kicked* out because I got upset about the solo thing. Now you're telling me you quit. But you're leaving out the part where you quit because you were too proud to take probation, which you totally deserved."

"The crowd loved—" Devane began.

Emerson held up one hand. "I don't want to do this again," she said. "Here's the deal. We all want you to come back, like I said. But we're not sure if Maddy and Gina will even let you now. We figure the only chance you have is to apologize to them and tell them you're willing to do the probation. It's not like it will be forever."

Devane opened her mouth, but she didn't know what to say. That *never* happened.

"I'll back you up," Emerson added. "I'll tell them *I* want you there. And if I want you there, it has to be cool with everyone else, right?"

Get her.

"Thanks for being willing to do me such a huge favor," Devane snapped. "I wouldn't need your help getting back into the group if you'd kept your mouth shut in the first place, remember? I'd still be in."

"Have you told yourself that so many times you really believe it?" Emerson asked. "Do you just think because what you did when you changed the choreography was amazing and the crowd loved it that Gina and Maddy wouldn't care? Don't you remember that day in class when you did little things—like that cross-legged flare when Gina told us to do a single? She wasn't happy about it. *I* didn't yell at you that day, and she was still mad at you."

"Do you want some water?" Devane asked. She wanted some water. "It comes out of the sink. You've probably never tasted that kind before," she added.

"No, I've said what I have to say." Emerson stood up. "I'm not going to beg you. I know you don't like me. I don't especially like you, either. But we all want you in the group. You're one of the best dancers."

"One of?" Devane asked automatically, her mind still on that day in class, on how Gina made her stay after to lecture her about not being a team player.

"All you have to do is swallow your pride and apologize and just take the probation," Emerson said as she headed to the door.

Devane shook her head. "You just said I'm one of the best dancers. That means I deserved a solo. I was trying to take some of what was mine." She shook her head again. Too many thoughts were rising up. Pricking at her. "I don't need the group to get what I want. I can do it on my own."

Emerson turned back to face her. "That's your whole problem. You want to do everything on your own. You want one big solo. You're a diva, even though you say you aren't."

"And proud of it," Devane told her.

"Well, Gina and Maddy don't want divas. They want team players," Emerson said, voice calm, her blue eyes serious. "And I'm offering to be on your team. Everyone else is, too. So what are you going to do about it?"

CHAPTER 11

Two days later the same judges were talking to the same—well, almost the same—messed-up people. Dr. Phil was still yelling, *"What are you thinkin'?"* Devane was still on the couch.

Tamal walked past her, heading for the front door. "Where are *you* going?" she asked.

"Pickup basketball," he answered.

"Does Mom know? You're not supposed to just go roaming around."

Tamal turned around and stared at her. "I've been going every day this summer, so yeah, I think she knows. If it's any of your business."

Devane stood up. "Maybe I'll watch. It wouldn't hurt for somebody to make sure you go where you say you go."

Tamal put his hands on his hips. "Uh, na-nay-no," he said in a high voice. As if that sounded like her.

"You don't tell me where I can and can't go," Devane told him, keeping on her feet.

"Come on. No one's big sister watches them play," Tamal said. "And it's not on your calendar. Your three-year plan won't work out if you go. Or is the three-year plan flushed now?"

"No!" Devane told him. "I just have to revise it. I was thinking of making it a two-year plan. I don't think it should take three."

"All right. So, see, you don't have any time to waste watching b-ball. You have to revise or whatever." Tamal hurried out of the apartment and slammed the door. The boy always slammed the door. And he never remembered to lock it.

Devane sighed and started across the room. Her mother came through the door before Devane could reach it, the handles of several plastic grocery bags looped over each wrist. "Let me get some of those." Devane slid the bags off her mother's right hand.

"Thanks, boo." Her mother dumped her bags on the narrow kitchen counter. "I passed your brother on the stairs. He warned me that you were in a stinky mood, he called it, and that you've been in a stinky mood for days."

"I told him not to eat with his mouth open. Do you call that stinky?" Devane muttered. She put her bags on the counter and started to unload them. But the silence in the room started to feel like a weight pressing down on her. Why wasn't her mother talking? Why didn't she ask

Devane something?

"I don't understand why that girl Emerson would come over here the other day supposedly trying to help me when I busted in on her solo," Devane burst out, just to break the quiet. She couldn't breathe in all that quiet. "I wouldn't have done that. If she'd grabbed part of my solo, I'd have pulled out all her hair."

Devane's mother raised her eyebrows. "So you're saying her mama just raised her better than I raised you?"

"Well, I'd have wanted to pull her hair out," Devane corrected. "There's no way ballerina girl would really back me if I showed up at class and apologized. No one is that pure."

"Have you been studying mind reading during all that free time you've had now that you're not dancing?" her mother asked, putting three cans of Tamal's beloved SpaghettiOs in the cupboard.

Clearly her mother was on Emerson's side. Didn't she know that mothers were supposed to back the daughters? Always.

"But what if I go down there and she just laughs at me? What if she's just playing me? Trying to get some payback?" Devane asked. Even though it *was* hard to imagine Emerson doing that. She'd sounded so dead serious about the whole team thing. And Devane knew the girl wasn't that talented an actress.

"There are worse things than being laughed at," her mother said. Why couldn't her mama ever just say, *"Oh, poor baby, you just stay right here with me. I don't want you to get hurt"*?

Devane looked at the clock. It was just a little past the time she'd usually be leaving for class. "I'd usually be leaving for class right about now," she said.

Her mother kept on unpacking groceries. The silence started pushing down on Devane again.

"Maybe I'll go down there." Devane wadded one of the empty plastic bags into a ball.

Her mother didn't say, "I think you should," or, "No, I won't allow it." There was just that silence.

"Would that be all right?" Devane asked.

Her mother smiled. "I think that would be very all right."

M.J., Fridge, and Max stared at Emerson as she walked into class. But it wasn't a bad kind of staring. A little intense, but not bad. "What did she say?" M.J. asked.

"Wait. Wait. Wait, wait, wait. I want to hear this, too!" Sophie called, rushing into the room with Sammi. Sophie immediately hurried over to Emerson and bumped shoulders with her. Emerson noticed that Sammi was watching the two of them, and she looked a little hurt.

"I went over there and—"

"You should wait a few minutes more," Sophie said. "You're just going to have to repeat everything when everyone else gets here."

"So what?" Max exclaimed. "We need to know now." She gave a little hop. Like an exclamation point. "If you don't want to repeat everything, I'll do it for you."

"There's not that much to repeat," Emerson said. "I went over there, and I told her what we all decided I'd tell her—that we wanted her back in the group and that we thought if she apologized to Gina and Maddy and agreed to take the probation, they'd let her."

"What did she say?" ill papi asked as he and Chloe joined the group.

"She basically said that she didn't need the group and that she was proud to be a diva," Emerson admitted.

Chloe snorted. "Of course she did."

"Maybe I didn't say the right thing—" Emerson began.

"She probably expected you to come over with offerings of little dog coats and M&M's with the green ones picked out. She probably expected you to beg her," Sophie said.

Emerson wasn't sure. Devane talked big. But there was something a little I-am-the-great-and-powerful-Oz about the whole conversation. Like maybe the real Devane was hiding somewhere behind all the I-am-the-great-and-powerful-diva stuff.

"So now what do we do?" M.J. asked.

"I don't think there's anything else we can do," Emerson admitted. *Unless I can find a little Toto dog to rip away the curtain so I can talk to the real Devane. If there is one,* she thought.

"What'd she say?" Becca asked as soon as she came through the door. She was wearing a shirt with a big sheep on it that said, "Ewe aren't fat. Ewe are fluffy."

Emerson gave her short report again. Then once more when Ky showed up, dribbling his basketball, with the twins and Rachel right behind him. She had to stop herself from automatically launching into the spiel when Gina entered.

"I want to remind you all of what I said last time. No goofing around," Gina immediately called out. She shot a look at Sophie. "I want focus. If I don't get it, I'm sending people home. I want no interruptions."

But five minutes later, she got one. A big one.

Devane walked into the room, and everyone stopped dancing. Gina looked ready to order them all out—forever. Then she turned around and saw Devane, too.

Devane started toward Gina. Emerson's breath caught in her chest. What if all of them were wrong? What if an apology wasn't good enough for Gina? What if she yelled at Devane?

Then Devane stopped. What was she doing? Had she changed her mind? Was she leaving?

Devane turned toward the class. "I just wanted to tell everyone I'm sorry about what I did at the show," she said, her voice loud and clear. "We all worked on the routine together, and I could have messed it up for all of you." She looked over at Gina. "I wasn't acting like I was part of a team."

She finally gets it, Emerson thought. *She's not just saying the words. She gets it.*

Devane turned her gaze to Emerson and looked at her for a long moment, her expression unreadable. Finally she added, "The only reason I didn't screw it up for you is because Emerson covered for me." It sounded like it was a little hard for her to get the words past her teeth. "You have to be a good dancer to cover like that."

Emerson blinked. She was starting to think she really had ended up in the Land of Oz. Because Devane had just paid her a compliment. In front of everyone.

Devane needed air. Real outside air. She couldn't stand in the practice room in front of everyone. She bolted. She couldn't even keep her dignity and hold herself to a walk until she was out of the room. She just bolted. Like an embarrassed child. Humiliating. But she couldn't stop running until she reached the sidewalk outside the studio.

Then she took deep, deep breaths, trying to feel, just

trying to feel like Devane again. When she did, she realized that Devane felt . . . pretty good. She hadn't planned on giving a speech to the whole group like she had. She was just going to apologize to Gina. But when she'd seen everybody standing there, she realized she really had risked wrecking something that was just as important to all of them as it was to her. Or almost as important. So she had to step up and say what she'd said.

And after she had, she couldn't stand to be in that room one more second. She couldn't make herself beg to be let back in the group. Even though now, she was willing to do her probation time.

"Devane!"

She turned toward the voice and saw Gina hurrying over to her. Cleary Devane wasn't done with her stepping up. *Whatever Gina has to say, you have to listen. You owe her that,* Devane told herself.

"I'm glad I caught you. I wanted to tell you I was really impressed by what you did in there. It took guts."

Devane's mouth opened, but she couldn't come up with any words. The second time that had happened in a week. *A miracle,* she could imagine Tamal shouting.

"It would have been easier for you to come to me or Maddy when we were alone. To say your piece in front of the whole class—that really showed me something. That you care about the team," Gina continued. "It showed real growth, Devane."

"Thank you," Devane managed to get out.

"You're the kind of person Maddy and I want in the Performance Group," Gina continued.

All the saliva in Devane's mouth evaporated. The moisture seemed to travel to her palms, which were suddenly sweating.

"And I suspect from the reaction of the class when you walked through the door that they all feel the same way." Gina gave Devane a long look. "So what do you say, Devane? You'd still be on probation, but you'd be part of the team."

Devane swallowed hard. "Yes."

A question popped into Devane's head. *Am I going to be off probation for the Disney World show? Because you* know *you need me for that one.*

But she didn't say any of that. She wasn't Tamal-dumb. "Yes," she told Gina again.

"What are you waiting for?" Gina grinned. "Go get changed for class. Everybody's waiting for you."

CHAPTER 12

Sammi rushed down the hall after Sophie and Emerson. Sophie and Emerson. Sophie and Emerson. At Hip Hop Kidz it was always Sophie and Emerson. Half the time Sophie acted like she didn't even know Sammi when they were at the dance studio. Forget about that they were sisters.

"Soph!" Sammi grabbed her by the elbow. "I need you." She turned to Emerson. "You should go ahead and change. I need to talk to my sister about . . . sister stuff."

"Okay," Emerson answered. "See you." She gave them a little wave and continued on toward the locker room.

"What?" Sophie asked, all grouchy. "Emerson and I were talking."

"I need you to be ill papi," Sammi said.

"What?" Sophie said again, more loudly.

"I decided that today, I'm taking it up a level with him," Sammi explained. "I'm going to ask him out. Maybe he's shy—"

"I don't think ill papi is shy," Sophie interrupted.

"You never know. Some really cute guys are shy. It's like they're unaware of their own cuteness and the power it gives them," Sammi answered. "Or maybe he's clueless. Maybe he hasn't figured out that I've been trying to get his attention."

"I don't think ill papi is clueless," Sophie said.

"Whatever his deal is, asking him out will solve it. If he's shy—he doesn't have to ask me. If he's clueless—this will totally spell it out. If he's a slow mover—this will speed things up." Sammi had thought all this through last night while soaking in a tub full of Lush Karma bubbles, which were handmade and kind of expensive. So she only used the bubble bar when she had heavy-duty thinking to do.

"You're doing it, so do it," Sophie said. "I don't see why you need me."

"I told you, I need you to be ill papi," Sammi explained. "I need a practice run. We have to do it fast because I want to catch him before he leaves. I'll go insane if I have to wait until next time to ask him. Okay, so you're ill papi."

"I'm ill papi," Sophie repeated, her voice flat. Was she trying to sound like him? Because she definitely didn't sound like happy Sophie.

"Hey, ill papi." Sammi didn't do a hair flip of any degree. Her nightmare had freaked her out too much. "The new Will Ferrell movie is opening this weekend. I can't wait to see it. Do you want to go with me?"

"I don't really like Will Ferrell," Sophie said.

Good. She was giving Sammi a chance to rehearse some possible negative responses.

"Oh, well, there's lots of other fun stuff out," Sammi told Sophie slash ill papi. "Are you into action movies? Or horror? I like horror. To me it's like a roller coaster. I like to get all scared but be totally safe." She did a quick arm touch. She hadn't done an arm touch with ill papi before, but they were good for telling a boy, "I like you."

Sophie didn't reply. "Come on," Sammi urged.

"I can't do this," Sophie said. "I don't know how to think like him. I'll see you in the locker room."

"Okay." At least Sophie had helped her get warmed up, Sammi thought. She did an ill papi scan and spotted him heading for the main exit. "Ill papi, wait up!" she cried.

He turned around, and Sammi got to him as fast as she could without breaking out of a walk. "Hey, that new Will Ferrell movie is coming out this weekend. Do you want to go with me?"

"No."

That was it. Just no.

And ill papi had left the building.

Sammi hadn't even considered that possibility in the bathtub.

Sophie sat in the locker room waiting for Sammi. She used the time to practice her I'm-so-happy-for-you smile. She practiced it so many times that her lips and jaw were starting to ache. Even her teeth hurt. But when Sammi came prancing in there, talking about the big plans she and ill papi had made, Sophie wanted to be able to smile. Sammi was her sister, and Sophie was going to be happy for her. Even if it felt like someone was pulling her fingernails out.

The locker room door swung open. There went a fingernail. Sophie braced herself.

But Sammi had tears in her eyes when she threw herself down on the bench opposite her sister. "What happened?" Sophie cried.

"He said no! Ill papi said no!" Sammi burst out, getting curious looks from some of the other girls. "That's all. Just no. I got one word from him, Soph."

"That's harsh," Sophie said. She reached over and grabbed Sammi's hand. But she felt a smile pulling at her lips. Probably just because she'd been doing so much smile practice.

Or maybe because it felt kind of fair somehow. Sammi already had the Hip Hop Kidz Performance Group—at least she was getting really close, with Devane not being able to perform right now. Did she have to have *everything* Sophie wanted?

Emerson leaned over and let her hair fall over her face, then started to brush it out. The simple motion felt good after the hard workout of class.

"Hey, Blondie."

Emerson straightened up, flipping back her hair. She found Devane standing in front of her. No surprise. No one else called her Blondie. Or Ballerina.

"I'm glad it worked out with Gina," Emerson said. And she was. Sort of. But class would always have more tension in it with Devane around.

"I wanted to give you a separate apology," Devane said in a rush.

"That's okay. You kind of already did," Emerson told her.

"Not about the solo thing. About what I said to you that first day. That you weren't in the right place," Devane explained. "Remember?"

Emerson definitely remembered. She'd been feeling out of place anyway. She'd only been in class a few months. She hardly talked to anyone—just Sophie—and back then she hardly even knew Sophie. And she was much more a ballet dancer than a b-girl. What Devane had said had been like a slap. "I remember," was all she said.

"I remember, too!" Sophie came around the corner and

joined in the conversation. "I figured you were just trying to psych out the competition before the non-audition audition. I kept waiting for you to tell me my puppy had just died or something. But you didn't say anything to me. I was insulted. I guess you didn't think I was good enough to bother playing head games with."

Devane and Emerson laughed.

"Well, anyway, I was wrong," Devane told Emerson. "You pretty much kept up with me at the show. And if you didn't belong here, you wouldn't have been able to do that."

Emerson smiled. Devane was definitely still a little bit of a diva. "Thanks, I guess."

Max's head appeared over the top of the row of lockers. She had to be part spider. She could climb anything. "Hey, you guys, we're meeting for pizza on the corner." Her head disappeared.

"Do you think that means I'm invited?" Emerson asked Sophie.

"Absolutely," Sophie said.

"Do you want to go, Soph?" Sammi called from the bathroom. "Dad's going to be a little late picking us up anyway."

"Sure." She looked at Devane. "You coming?"

"You should come," Emerson said.

"I could eat a slice." Devane held up one finger. "But know this. I'm going to do whatever it takes to get off probation. And I'm going to do whatever it takes to get myself a solo in the Disney World show."

"*Whatever* it takes?" Emerson repeated. Had she been wrong about Devane actually getting it?

"Not like that," Devane said. "I just mean that I'm going to work my butt off. Every class I'm going to bring it. So I'm warning you now, both of you—and everybody else in this locker room—you better bring it, too, if you don't want to end up as one of Divine Devane's backup dancers."

Emerson nodded. "Consider it brought."

WORD UP:

Get the moves with these def-initions . . .

DEF-initions

1990: A rotating handstand.

Bronco: A move where the dancer falls to his/her hands, kicks up the feet, then jumps back up to a standing position.

Clowning: A mix of popping, locking, break dancing, and African tribal dance.

Cross-legged flare: A more difficult version of a flare done with crossed legs.

Eggbeater: A sustained backspin with legs in the air and hands high on the hips.

Flare: A move where the dancer is on the floor with the weight on his/her hands and swings the legs in big circles in front of and behind the arms.

Float: The dancer balances on his/her hands with the body horizontal (legs sometimes bent).

Kip up: A move where the dancer is flat on his/her back, rolls backward, kicks out the feet, and lands upright.

Locking: A jerky style where dancers move through a series of ultra-quick poses.

Popping: A style where dancers move through poses in a more fluid way than in locking.

Slide: Sliding across the floor on some part of the body.

Wassup, Peeps?

I've been in Hip Hop Kidz for about 4 years now. I'm currently 17 years old. Thinking back, I have had some awesome times with HHK, like the time we went to Connecticut to perform in their annual parade, or when we were invited to be in the Miami segment of the Macy's Thanksgiving Day Parade, and all those trips to New York. Even the local events are cool because I enjoy what I do and I get to do it with people I love.

When I first started with HHK I was about 13 years old and I was an okay dancer . . . okay, let me stop lying . . . I was bad (haha). I felt very self-conscious about it—kind of the way a lot of the kids in the book feel about certain things. Like the way Sophie feels about her weight, Emerson feels about being rich, and Devane feels about being poor. I guess it's natural to feel like you're different from everyone else in the beginning. But my instructors, Dee and Suzy, encouraged me to stay with HHK because they saw that I had potential. That was around the same time that my family wasn't doing its best financially. But Suzy believed in me and allowed me to be on a full scholarship. Through the years, I worked really hard and got better and better and moved up the ladder until I reached where I am now— "The Professionals." (Has a nice ring to it, doesn't it?) One thing that I can say for sure is that if it wasn't for Suzy's encouragement, I would not be doing the things I do today.

Besides everything I do with HHK, I have also branched off to do other stuff with the entertainment "biz." I have performed in many live music award shows, modeled and acted in commercials, and been in some music videos. And it all started because I was looking for a chance to make friends, get some exercise, and just be able to perform. I found all that and more through HHK. I have grown in my abilities, I make nice money for a teenager in "the biz," and my mom, sister, and I live comfortably. I'm so glad I stuck with HHK, even though it was hard in the beginning. I guess what I'm trying to say is that you shouldn't let feeling different get in the way of doing what you love.

Sean, age 17